LOST GIRLS

ADRIFT!

LOST GIRLS

LOST GIRLS

ADRIFT!

Linda Williams Aber

AN
APPLE
PAPERBACK

SCHOLASTIC INC.
New York Toronto London Auckland Sydney

With special thanks to:
my mother for showing me the Abaco Islands;
Hal, Corey, and Kip Aber for allowing me time
to get lost in The Lost Girls*; Ann Reit for being*
a kind and good editor; Louise Colligan for
friendly encouragement; and Huzzy, wherever
she may be, for writing her name in the cement
on one of the Abaco Islands.

ISBN 0-590-43536-1

12 11 10 9 8 7 6 5 4 3 2 1   1 2 3 4 5 6/9

Printed in the U.S.A.   40

First Scholastic printing, July 1991

For
those who love adventure

Preface

A warm wind breathes softly over the tiny island known, by any who know it at all, as Chilas Cay. The tall casuarina trees bend to the breeze and forget to come back. The pose is permanent. They lean to the northwest and stop, as if listening for some sound or sigh from someone, anyone. It is a sound heard only once on Chilas Cay. This island has long ago been lost to those who sail the turquoise waters of the Atlantic Ocean where the clusters of Abaco Islands lie mostly empty, mostly forgotten.

It was more than two hundred years ago that the last visitor came to the island. A Greek sea captain sailing from the port of Limnia off the island of Chios washed ashore on the storm-battered boards of the schooner *Kayasku*. The whipping winds that took his ship spared his life and delivered him safely to the bright, white sands of undiscovered beach.

Alone and unafraid, this man lived off the

fruits of the island and the fish of the sea. Day after day, month after month, he watched and waited for the tide to bring in another piece of the *Kayaska*, and another, and another, until at last a new boat could be made. Tying the boards together with ropes made of sea-soaked sisal plants, Captain Dimitrios Chilas christened his rough vessel *Little Kayaska*, and sailed safely to Green Turtle Cay, where he told his story, and where the story has been told ever since.

1.
The Girls

Mother!"

No answer.

"Mother! I'm talking to you!" Allison McKinney stood with her weight on one foot while the other foot tapped impatiently up and down. She could never get her mother to simply answer her. Taking time out from yelling, Allison leaned into her dresser mirror and stared absently at her tanned face, her thick, long, crimped dark-brown hair, and her green eyes, which she'd just finished outlining in blue eye pencil. As she fluffed up her hair for the umpteenth time that morning, she tried to get her mother's attention away from the telephone.

"Mother!" she yelled again.

"I'm on the telephone, Allison, *dear*," her mother shouted back from somewhere in another part of the large three-story house. Thick carpeting covered all the floors and absorbed some of the shrieking that always seemed to be going on in the McKinney house. Allison and her mother had always shouted instead of talked. It seemed the only way to get each other to listen.

"Well, can't you get off the telephone for one second just to help me pack? I don't know what to bring on a boat." She looked helplessly around at the piles of brand-new outfits that covered the twin canopy beds, the top of her desk, and the chair.

She heard her mother saying in an annoyed tone, "Well, I guess she's not going to give up. I'll have to go rescue her. Kids. Talk to you later."

The phone was slammed down, and Allison heard her mother's thonged sandals slapping, slapping against her heels as she stomped up the stairs to Allison's room.

It was the perfect room for a fourteen-year-old who loved boys almost as much as she loved makeup. Everything was baby-blue. Baby-blue bedspreads, baby-blue canopies, baby-blue curtains, baby-blue wallpaper. Pictures of boys were on every flat surface. Boys she'd met at school. Boys she'd met at the pool. Boys she'd met at the mall. Boys she'd met wherever she went. Allison guessed there wasn't a place in the world she could go and not meet boys. She didn't know how she did it; she just did.

"Allison! When I'm on the phone I don't need

4

your voice shouting into my other ear!" Mrs. McKinney yelled, causing the hair rollers on the top of her head to bounce a little.

"Well, you're always on the phone, so when am I supposed to ask you anything?" Allison yelled back. "All I want to do is get this stupid suitcase packed for this stupid boat trip you're making me go on."

"It's not a boat trip," her mother corrected. "It's a cruise. A sailing cruise, and you're going because it will broaden your experience. You can't spend every waking minute of your summer at the mall, you know. Here. Put these in there." She reached into Allison's walk-in-closet and pulled out three pairs of sandals, a pair of low dress heels, and a pair of blue flats with rhinestones and silver star studs at the toe.

Allison just watched as her mother worked like a tornado pulling out more and more things for the suitcase. Three bathing suits, three matching bathing suit cover-ups, five shorts-and-tops outfits, three pants outfits, electric rollers, a curling iron, hair dryer, several nightgowns, two sweaters, and a jacket. In a separate makeup case her mother put bottles of lotions, creams, compacts of eye shadow, tubes of lipstick, eyeliner pencils, mascara, hairspray, mousse, gel, toothpaste, and a toothbrush.

"There!" said her mother proudly. "Now, do I know how to pack or do I know how to pack?"

Well, you should, thought Allison to herself, *since you're always going away!*

Mrs. McKinney threw in a handful of barrettes, hair clips, ribbons, and headbands as an after-thought.

"Mother," groaned Allison. "It's only going to be a bunch of girls."

"Well, you never know. And you always want to look your best no matter what." She looked in Allison's mirror as she said this and smoothed the skin on her neck. "Now, hurry up and finish whatever else you have to do, because the van will be here to pick you up any minute. You shouldn't have waited until now to start packing, I told you that. You have to be all ready." She shook her head in annoyance, the way she always did with Allison.

"I *am* all ready," Allison barked. To herself she thought, *The only good thing about this trip will be getting away from my mother. And isn't it too bad it's only for a week?*

A horn honking outside interrupted the yelling and shouting.

"Well, there. I told you so. Now the van is here. You take the makeup case, and I'll get the driver to come in for the suitcase." Her mother moved quickly down the stairs, her sandals slapping her heels all the way out the front door where a red van with the words *Windswept Sailing Cruises* painted in white was parked. It stood empty and waiting for the first passenger, Allison McKinney.

In less than five minutes the suitcase was loaded into the back of the van, and Allison took a seat in the middle section of seats right by a window. Her mother gave a quick kiss to the air somewhere near Allison's cheek. She handed Allison an envelope. "It's from your father," she said. "He called and said to be sure to tell you to have a good trip, and he's sorry he had to be out of town when you were leaving."

Allison knew what would be in the envelope. Money. How many envelopes had been handed to her with an apology for not being able to "be there"?

The driver, a cheerful fat man who didn't need the suspenders he wore to hold up his pants, closed the door and took his seat. Before the van had driven away, Allison's mother was already back inside the house picking up the phone to make another call.

Allison stuffed the envelope into her canvas bag without even looking at it. Ignoring the flat Florida scenery outside her window, she stared straight ahead. A whole week, she thought. And then thinking of her mother she wondered again, Is a week even long enough?

The red van turned down a narrow sandy road and bumped along in front of a row of small cinder-block houses all the same shape, but painted different pastel colors. It pulled to a stop in front of the neatest house on the row. Blue cornflowers sprouted out of white window boxes, drawing any passing person's eye right to the pale yellow house at the end of the row. This time the driver didn't have to honk the horn. Libby Hunt stood bouncing up and down with excitement next to her aunt Alice. Libby's naturally curly red hair was pulled up into a topknot and held with an orange polka-dotted scrunchy band that matched the mass of orange freckles on her round face.

"Oooo! Aunt Alice!" squealed the plumpish girl. "It's here! I can't believe I'm really going!" Then suddenly her eyes, which matched the cornflowers in the window boxes, looked up at the woman next to her. "But are you sure, sure, *sure* you'll be all right without me?" She turned to the softly rounded woman in the flowered housedress and hugged her as tightly as she could. "I don't like to leave you," she whispered.

"Now, Libby." The grandmotherly woman smiled kindly. "Don't you worry about me. I'll be just fine. That's not saying I won't miss my girl. But I'll be fine. This is my birthday present to you, and it's something I've been saving up for for a long time. When a girl turns twelve she's got to do something special. And this is sure to be something special."

The driver was out of the van now. "Your first trip alone?" he asked the happy-faced girl.

"Yup," answered Libby cheerfully. "And it's a present from my aunt Alice." She beamed at the woman who had been like a mother and father to her for the past five years since both her parents had been killed in a car accident.

The sailing cruise was going to be her first trip anywhere since her parents had died. Ever since then she'd always been too afraid to leave her aunt. That feeling of coming home from a field trip and hearing the terrible news of her parents' deaths never left her. She felt that if she never left Aunt Alice, there'd be no chance of coming home to bad news again.

"You've got to let go a little, Libby," Aunt Alice had told her. "I want you to be free. And as long as you have fear keeping you a prisoner you'll never be free."

After days of discussion and changing her mind back and forth again and again, Libby finally gathered her courage and agreed to go on the trip.

The driver was waiting patiently to help Libby into the van. Her small, blue nylon, zippered suitcase was already packed in the back, and the man stood holding the door open. Libby gave one last hug and kiss to her aunt and then climbed into the open van. She was startled to see another girl already inside. She was even more surprised to see the girl deliberately turn her head the other way and look out the window without even acknowledging Libby's happy "Hello!"

Oh, well, thought Libby. Maybe she's just shy.

Forgetting the other girl for the moment, Libby rolled down the window on her side and leaned her head out toward Aunt Alice. The woman reached a hand up and gave Libby's outstretched hand a trio of squeezes. Libby squeezed back four times.

I love you.

I love you, too.

It was their silent signal to each other.

"Don't look so worried, Libby," her aunt said sweetly. "A week will be gone before you know it!"

"Sure it will," said Libby with an uncertain smile. She waved good-bye to Aunt Alice until she could no longer see the flowers on her dress or the cornflowers against the house. See you in a week, Libby thought to herself.

Sarah Southard tried to put a protective arm around her younger sister, but Annie slipped out of the hold. It wasn't that she didn't like her older sister. Even with two years difference between them, Sarah had always treated her like an equal. She had always been perfectly nice to her. Perfectly sweet. Perfectly understanding.

Perfectly perfect. From her perfectly straight blonde hair to her perfectly tanned, tall body, Sarah Southard was, in Annie's opinion, too perfect.

"What's the matter, Anniekins?" Sarah smiled too sweetly at her eleven-year-old sister. "I think you look wonderful. That new red headband really shows up against your hair."

Annie looked out of the corner of her eye and caught her reflection in the mirror. Wonderful? she thought to herself. What she really means is 'Wonderful for *you*, Annie.'

Behind her own reflection, Annie saw her sister busily putting away the things she'd decided not to bring on the sailing cruise. That was another perfect thing about Sarah. "You're even a perfect packer," Annie muttered.

"Daddy showed me how to make everything fit without getting wrinkled," Sarah explained, although Annie already knew their father had spent the whole evening before going over all kinds of things with Sarah. First he taught her how to pack, then he showed her all the nautical charts and traced the route they'd be taking on the cruise. Then he talked on and on about his sailing days and all the races he'd won against his old college buddies. Since he wasn't really talking to Annie, Annie had just tuned it all out. She guessed that was why her suitcase looked a mess.

11

"Here," Sarah said, coming over to Annie's overflowing suitcase. "Let me help you fold some of these things better. They'll all fit if you get them folded right. Everything will look fine in a jiffy." As she talked she rolled some things and carefully folded others. "There. See? It's better already." In no time Sarah had made three neat stacks of the shorts, shirts, nightgowns, and underwear in Annie's suitcase.

"Thanks," said Annie. "It looks perfect."

"Are my girls ready?" sang the happy voice of the girls' mother as she glided into the room they shared. "That's my good girl, Sarah. Are you helping Annie get her things toge — " She stopped in midsentence. "Annie! Your hair looks dreadful! Sarah, can't you help her fix it? It looks all straggly."

"That's because it is straggly," Annie said, not even defending herself. "It's mousy brown and straggly." Annie tore the new red headband out of her hair.

"Oh, Annie, honey. I am sorry. I didn't mean to hurt your feelings. It's just that it needs a little brushing, I think."

"I did brush it," Annie argued, putting the headband back on.

"Well, brush a little more, sweetheart," Mrs. Southard said, pushing back the stray hairs that wouldn't stay under the band. "Now, here," she

12

continued, handing each of them a wrapped package. "This is just a little *bon voyage* present that will come in handy, I think."

The two sisters opened their presents at the same time.

"Oh!" said Sarah delightedly as she held up a beautiful turquoise beach towel with a white sailboat pictured on it. "I love it! Thank you, Mom!"

"I saw the color and just had to get it for you. It matches your eyes exactly." Mrs. Southard beamed at her beautiful oldest daughter.

Annie unfolded her towel. "What does mine match?" she said sarcastically as she held up a mustard-colored towel with a brown bear sitting in a green-and-white-striped beach chair. It was possibly the ugliest beach towel she'd ever seen. But, she thought, she should be used to things like this by now. Sarah and her blue eyes always got the pretty-colored things. Even when they were very little and wore matching dresses, Sarah got the blue dress and Annie got the pea-green. Whenever she questioned it, she always heard the same thing.

"Well, you've got that olivey skin," her mother would explain. "You can wear those colors no one else can wear."

"And no one else *wants* to wear," Annie would answer back.

13

"Here," Sarah said, handing her new towel over to Annie. "This one matches your bathing suit."

"What bathing suit?" asked Annie.

"Mine from last year. You know the one you always liked so much. I'm sure it'll fit you this year." Sarah gave Annie a hug and pushed the towel on her. "Please take it."

"Oh," said their mother, "but the sailboat was for you. . . ."

Before Sarah could answer, a familiar whistled tune drifted through the hallway, followed by a boisterous, "Where are my two favorite girls?"

It was their father. And Annie was sure she knew the truth. Only one of them was his favorite, and it wasn't her. It was a surprise when he came and put his arm around her shoulder as he spoke to both of them.

"Well, you lovely ladies, I wish I could go with you. But try to have a good time without me now, won't you?" He laughed at his own joke.

"Oh, Daddy," said Sarah, giving her father a hug. "I really will miss you."

"And I'll miss both of you," he said, putting an arm around each of the girls.

The honking horn out front broke up the huggers. "They're here!" shouted Sarah, her blonde hair flying out behind her as she dashed to the window to look out. "It's the van! The *Windswept* van is here!"

Mr. Southard closed the two suitcases and carried them downstairs and out to the van. Mrs. Southard and the girls followed, exchanging hugs and kisses all the way. All four of the Southard family members had tears in their eyes as they waved good-bye and called out last minute *I'll miss you*'s and *I love you*'s.

Once inside the van, Sarah introduced herself and Annie to the other two girls who were already seated. Annie hardly noticed who they were. All she seemed to be able to see was Sarah being "Miss Perfect," and it was obvious even the scowling-faced girl named Allison scowled less at Sarah than she did at her. The other girl, Libby, was all smiles to both of them. Annie was just about to like her until she said too cheerfully, "Oh, you two are sisters?" And then to Annie, "You are so lucky to have an older sister, especially one as beautiful as yours."

A thought fluttered through Annie's mind. You want her? You can have her! I could live without her, that's for sure!

The thought was erased when Sarah ruffled her hair in her friendly, sisterly way and said, "Well, Anniekins, this is it! We're on our own. Really on our own."

* * *

The bathroom mirror was covered with a thick coating of steam from the shower. Instead of just wiping it away with the corner of her bath towel, Shawn Kallin quickly dried herself, slipped on a pair of peach-colored shorts and a matching tank top, and used the towel to wrap her waist-length brown hair turban-style on top of her head. Then she leaned over the sink and with her long index finger drew a picture on the mirror. She drew the ocean with the sun rising out of it, birds flying above it, and a sailboat gliding across it with sails full of wind. In the lower right-hand corner of her mirror drawing, she signed her work the way she signed all of her drawings, paintings, and poems. Just *Shawn*. She liked the way her signature looked without a middle or last name. That was how she liked to think of herself, as just beginning, with the middle and the end still to be filled in.

"Shawn," her bearded father had said during one of their many talks in his painting studio behind their house. "If you think of your life as an empty canvas, you'll see that how you fill that canvas is up to you. You can make it all one color and always know that the next stroke of the brush will be just like the one before it. Or you can fill your canvas with many different colors for a picture full of surprises."

She knew exactly what he meant, and she had already made up her mind that her life would be colorful and full of those surprises her father mentioned. Already her life was more colorful than the lives of most other fourteen-year-old girls she knew. Both her parents were artists. Her older brother, Tate, was a musician. She had always been surrounded by creative people, and she'd grown up in a house full of art, music, and books. These things were, as her mother said so often, "the bread and water of life."

This is what Shawn had thought about as she packed her oversized duffel bag the night before. In addition to the pair of well-worn jeans, black University-of-Paris sweatshirt, shorts, underwear, and other bare-minimum essentials, she filled half the bag with her art supplies, a notebook already half-filled with her own poetry, a tape player, and her favorite tape called *Watermark* by a singer who also used only her first name, Enya.

"Trés bien," Shawn had said to her black cat, Pablo, who sat quietly watching as she pulled the zipper across the top of the bag and secured it with two snapped flaps. "Filled with the bread and water of life, and some clothes besides!"

Pablo yawned, making Shawn feel the tiredness from her excitement about the sailing cruise she'd be leaving for the next morning. She slept soundly and woke up that morning rested and ready for the wonderful week out on the ocean with none of the distractions of everyday life. No television, no traffic. Nothing but beautiful sky, beautiful sea, and peace, she thought now as the last signs of her steam-drawing evaporated. "A whole week away from the real world!" For Shawn, who would always prefer her own world to the real one, the Windswept Sailing Cruise was sure to be a dream come true.

When the van arrived to pick her up, the dream was shattered slightly. As the girl called Sarah introduced herself and the other three girls already in the van, Shawn had only one thought: I just hope they'll all leave me alone.

The Florida sun did what it was famous for. It shone brilliantly, bouncing sparkling diamonds of light off the surface of the turquoise-blue water.

Huzzy Smyth stood straight and tall at the end of the weathered dock. She stood still, as the basin full of boats bobbed up and down at their moorings and bumped against the dock. The masts on the sailboats danced from side to side as the waves slapped the hulls of the boats, rocking them gently. Against the backdrop of the solid blue sky, Huzzy's smooth black skin made every detail of her slim silhouette stand out just as clearly as the unrigged masts. She had sleek black hair pulled back in a tight ponytail, long black eyelashes shading black velvet eyes, and a slightly turned-up nose over a full, heart-shaped mouth.

Born Harriet Eliza Smyth, Huzzy was "Huzzy" the minute her father saw her stretched to the full length of the tiny crib. And she was a Smyth through and through. Strong bones, straight back, long lean fingers, bright white smile, and a kinship to the sea rivaled only by that of the great green sea turtles for which her island home was named. All these characteristics were Smyth family traits. And the Smyth family had been a part of Green Turtle Cay's history "since the first conch was coaxed out of its shell and into the soup pot," Huzzy's grandfather used to brag.

Huzzy was the first Smyth to find work off-island. She left Green Turtle, but she didn't go far. Fort Lauderdale was not more than two hundred miles from the cluster of seven hundred islands known as the Abacos. Green Turtle Cay was one of the twenty-two occupied islands. The rest remained unsettled, unknown, unclaimed, or just too far out of reach from the normal sea routes traveled by boats or ships.

When word reached the people of Green Turtle that Windswept Sailing Cruises was looking for someone who really knew the Abaco Island waters to sail their newest vessel, Huzzy Smyth's name came to everyone's mind. No one knew the waters like Huzzy did. No one was quite so expert a sailor as she. It was the perfect job for her, she just knew it. At first the directors of Windswept worried that seventeen years old was too young to be a skipper, but when Huzzy showed how easily she handled the 39-foot sloop called *Sea Breeze*, the job was hers.

Huzzy had been sailing with her father all around Whale Cay Channel and through the Sea of Abaco since she was old enough to say "sail." Reading nautical charts came as easily to her as reading road maps did to other people. She knew she would be an expert skipper. The harder part of this job might be handling five girls who had never sailed before, girls from the mainland. That thought made Huzzy swallow hard.

She looked down at the clipboard she held in her left hand. Clipped to it was the passenger list for the cruise beginning June 12. Today. She'd read the names on the list again and again. Then she matched the names up with the pictures that came clipped to each girl's application. For the past week she'd studied those names and faces until she was sure she knew them. She tested herself silently one more time. Allison McKinney. Sarah and Annie Southard. Libby Hunt. Shawn Kallin.

Well, she thought, her confidence returning. That will be that. At least I've got their names.

She checked her yellow sport watch and saw that "her girls" were due to arrive exactly at that moment. And just then, the red Windswept van came rolling smoothly to a stop by the dock.

"Say hey, Huzzy!" the driver of the van called out the window in his jolly voice. "Beautiful day for a cruise, isn't it? Beautiful!"

"Hey, John," Huzzy called back with a smile. "It was a good trip?"

"Fine. Just fine," John replied, jumping down from the driver's seat. "And I've brought you a good group of girls. I'm sure you'll make sailors of them in no time." He laughed, and Huzzy thought she detected some hidden meaning in his statement.

John opened the side door of the van, and one by one Huzzy's girls stepped out. After being behind the tinted glass windows of the van the brightness of the sun made all of them squint. As Huzzy looked over the group John said she'd make sailors of in no time, she was struck by the fact that these five girls had come all this way together in the van and not one of them was speaking to the other. Even the two Southard girls, whom she recognized as the sisters, stood quiet as strangers on an elevator.

"Welcome to Windswept Sailing Cruises," Huzzy said in her friendly island accent. "I'm Huzzy Smyth, your skipper aboard the *Sea Breeze.*"

Huzzy talked over Allison McKinney's bored sigh and tried to ignore the tapping of the girl's foot as she seemed impatient with Huzzy's introduction.

Sarah Southard was the first to step forward, put out her hand, and introduce herself and her sister, Annie.

Libby Hunt was already over by the *Sea Breeze* looking up at the high mast and checking out how neatly the lines were coiled around the pilings.

Shawn Kallin introduced herself last and immediately went to the edge of the dock, threw back her long hair, and let the salty air blow softly across her cheeks. She closed her eyes and imagined herself already floating out to sea.

Huzzy checked her watch again and saw that it was time to board. John had lined up all their bags on the dock next to the boat, and Huzzy instructed each girl to carry her own bag on board. Allison groaned when she looked over at her bulging suitcase and the makeup case that had to weigh at least a ton.

"Do not worry, Allison," the skipper assured her, "you will be able to make two trips for your luggage."

Although they'd been practically silent the whole ride there, now that Huzzy was calling out instructions and telling them some of the safety rules to follow, the excitement of what

22

they were about to do really began to stir all of them.

"Can you believe we're going to be sailing on *that* for a whole week?" Libby bubbled, holding onto Annie's arm as if to keep her own feet on the ground.

Libby's enthusiasm started spreading, and Annie smiled her first smile of the day. "It is going to be so, so neat, isn't it?" Annie said to Libby.

"Come on, Anniekins," Sarah said. "You and Libby grab your bags and we'll be first on board. Coming, Shawn?" Sarah called out to the girl who looked like a commercial for a tropical island vacation as she stood, eyes closed, and hair blowing gently in the warm breeze.

Her trance broken, Shawn breathed deeply, smiled, and joined the group who were now climbing onto what would be their home away from home for the next week. Huzzy stood dockside, lending a hand to each girl as she stepped onto the rubber footpad on the deck of the boat. Allison was the last to board. Huzzy reached her hand out to steady her as she put one sandaled foot all the way over the side instead of onto the pad.

"I can manage myself," Allison said rudely. Unfortunately her foot slid out, sending her reeling backward. Huzzy caught her just before she hit the dock.

Allison stood up, smoothed her hair, and acting almost as though she'd planned to fall, she tried again. This time she accepted Huzzy's hand. "Thanks," was all she said when she was safely on the boat.

Huzzy climbed aboard easily and looked down at Allison's feet. "The sandals will be better in your suitcase, do you not think so?" Huzzy said in a firm but pleasant voice. "Rubber shoes will keep both feet down on these slippery decks."

Thinking of the heels and rhinestone-toed flats her mother had packed for her, Allison just said, "Yeah, right."

The other girls were already seated on the side benches as Huzzy had requested. Allison took the only seat left, next to Libby. "Are you all right?" the red-haired girl asked worriedly. "You really went flying!"

Allison didn't answer.

Before Libby could feel the sting of Allison's snub, Huzzy was handing out safety-tip sheets and a red-and-white Windswept Sailing Cruise tote bag to each girl. She moved down the row handing out the bags, which were filled with soaps, shampoo, stationery, pens, postcards of the *Sea Breeze* and the Abaco Islands, a chocolate bar for each night at sea, and a flashlight.

As the girls looked with curiosity through their complimentary gifts, Huzzy officially welcomed them. "On behalf of Windswept Sailing

Cruises, may I wish you sunny days and smooth-sailing nights." Then, looking over the group that would be hers for the whole week, Huzzy smiled her biggest smile and said, "Well, girls, let the adventure begin!"

2.
The *Sea Breeze*

Even Libby, who was happy living in a small, orderly house where there was a place for everything and everything in its place, thought the cabins on the *Sea Breeze* were a little too small. Certainly the information sheet they'd all been sent ahead of time had been right when it said, *The cabin space aboard* Sea Breeze *is cozy but small. For the comfort and convenience of all passengers, please keep baggage to a minimum.*

The *Sea Breeze* cabin area was divided into four sections. The bow section, which was, as Huzzy explained, the front of the boat, was strictly for storage. Two sections were sleeping quarters. The forward quarters had two beds, and the aft had four. Huzzy had assigned the beds in advance, putting Libby in the forward cabin with herself and the other four girls in the aft.

As the girls emptied their suitcases, Huzzy packed them neatly into the storage area. This was also where supplies were kept. There was a good surplus of batteries, candles, matches, paper goods, bottled water, saltwater purifying kits, canned foods, and other nonperishable goods. None of what was in there interested Allison. She bumped her head on the low doorway ceiling as she passed her suitcase full of useless shoes to Huzzy and turned to go back to her bunk. When she saw her bed, which had been clear, now covered with all her bottles of creams, makeup, hair gel, mousse, and hairspray, Allison folded her arms, tapped her right foot angrily and shouted, "All right, who moved my stuff?"

Sarah and Annie turned their attention from unpacking to Allison. "What do you mean, Allison?" Sarah asked.

"We didn't touch anything," Annie added. "We're too busy moving our own stuff to be moving your stuff," she said, going back to setting up her Windswept tote bag items on her assigned shelf.

"I had everthing set up on my shelf, and now it's here on the bed," Allison snarled.

Now Shawn turned around calmly and spoke slowly. "You had everything set up on *your* shelf and on *my* shelf. I'm afraid I need that shelf for my own things."

Annie and Sarah both tried to disappear in the small space. They exchanged looks and both saw that the other was thinking the same thing: "Let's just stay out of this!"

"And just where am I supposed to keep all these things?" Allison said, unfolding her arms and waving one of them over the array of bottles on the bed.

"You have a very pretty face, Allison," Huzzy said, stepping into the cabin — and the argument. "All this makeup is not very necessary on the ocean. You will find the fish are not so picky."

The other girls couldn't help but laugh. At first Allison opened her mouth to let out her rage. Then looking around at the others she decided to keep her thoughts to herself for the moment.

"You can have some of my space on my shelf," Libby volunteered, peeking her head into the other girls' cabin and hoping to be helpful.

Allison considered the offer, realized the inconvenience of going into the forward cabin for such essentials as eye shadow and mascara, and clicked her tongue against the roof of her mouth in an exasperated response. "Never mind," she said, sweeping up an armload of the stuff and overloading her own shelf.

Huzzy watched patiently as the annoyed girl stacked bottles on bottles. When Allison was finally finished, Huzzy's cheerful island accent softened the opinion she offered. "You know, Allison, with this arrangement these bottles of things for your face may tumble onto your head. Shall I put the things you don't need in your case with your shoes?"

Uh-oh, thought Annie. Now Huzzy is really going to get it!

"Come on, Annie. You, too, Libby," Sarah suggested to the two youngest members of the group. "Why don't we go into the galley and see what's what." She hurried the girls through the cabin doorway into the kitchen area, leaving Allison, Huzzy, and Shawn to finish the shelf problem by themselves.

"Huzzy . . ." Allison began as the three girls were on their way out. "I didn't plan to change my whole life-style on this boat ride!"

"And it is not my plan to try to make you," Huzzy answered. "But it *is* my plan to keep you safe from harm, even if it is only a hit on the head with a bottle of lotion!" She held out an open hand. "It is better to put these things away, yes?"

Shawn watched Huzzy with admiration. If it had been *her* talking to Allison, she would have just let the bottles fall where they may. If the target they hit happened to be the stubborn girl's head, well, it would have been her own fault! But Shawn noticed Huzzy's calm patience and recognized the importance of that quality in a leader of such a mixed group as this one.

She would have preferred to share the forward cabin with Huzzy instead of with this spoiled, overly made up girl.

Allison was picking through the things on her shelf, choosing only two small items to hand over to Huzzy. Removing one eye shadow compact and a tube of lip gloss didn't help the crowding on the shelf, but Huzzy accepted the compromise gesture and went to put the things away in Allison's suitcase. When she had left the two girls alone, Allison sniffed, "Next time you need something of mine moved, I'd appreciate it if you'd ask."

Shawn focused her yellow-brown eyes on Allison's green ones and simply said, "It's going to be a long week, Allison." Then she straightened her paintbrushes, pencils, and sketch pads on her shelf, put on her black sunglasses, and walked through the doorway, past the other girls in the galley, and up the three steps to the main deck.

Allison just shrugged off Shawn's parting words and picked up a pocket mirror. She checked her makeup, picky fish or no picky fish, then fluffed up her hair and stepped over the threshold into the galley. Sarah and Libby were busily opening cabinets, looking into compartments, and exploring every inch of the kitchen area.

Annie had already decided that she was not

about to be treated like the littlest little sister by both Sarah and Libby. The two of them were already acting as though Libby were more Southard than Hunt. From the moment the red-haired girl had gotten in the van, Annie had a feeling she was going to be hanging all over Sarah. Well, let her, thought the plain-faced girl jealously. Annie had left them to go up on deck.

"Where are you going, Anniekins?" Sarah had called after her.

"And don't call me Anniekins all the time!" Annie called back as she disappeared up the steps to the deck above.

Sarah started to follow her sister, but she stopped when Libby squealed, "Look! Even the dishes are smaller than normal size. This will be like playing house!"

Allison rolled her eyes upward and groaned.

Sarah turned back to Libby and saw what the girl was talking about. Inside the undersized kitchen cabinets were perfect stacks of six of everything — dinner plates, bowls, cups and saucers, dessert plates, and plastic cups. All of the dishes had the words *Windswept Sailing Cruises* in red letters and the sailboat logo on them. So did the buoy-shaped salt and pepper shakers, the pot holders that hung on magnets over the stove, the paper napkins, the hand soaps at the small sink, the place mats on the Formica dining table, and even the wall clock.

Allison walked over to the small refrigerator and pulled open the door. Suddenly even she was laughing. "Check this out," she said, pointing to a whole shelf full of cans of soft drinks.

Libby read the words on the label of one of the cans: *"Windswept Cola."*

"I guess the only thing that hasn't been swept up by Windswept is us!" joked Sarah. "Better not sit down, Libby, or someone might come and paint a Windswept sailboat on you, too."

All three girls were laughing when Huzzy stepped through the doorway carrying two more things with the Windswept name and logo on them: a flag and something Huzzy called a "telltale."

"It is a wind vane," the skipper said. "We must hang it up with the flag at the head of the mast. Now it is cast-off time. Shall we go up?" She headed for the steps. "There will be plenty of time later to be below deck. Right now, come up top to see a beautiful sight. I think you will agree there is nothing more beautiful than to see the shore grow smaller and smaller as we leave it far behind us. Then you will really feel the excitement of being free on the ocean. Come. This is something not to miss." Huzzy's long legs took the four steps two at a time, and Sarah, Libby, and Allison were right behind her.

Up on deck, Sarah noticed right away that Annie and Shawn were standing down at the stern of the boat where Shawn was pointing to a hungry pelican perched on one of the pilings and swallowing a fish whole. Annie said something to Shawn that the others couldn't hear because of the breeze, and whatever she said made Shawn put an arm around her and give a warm squeeze to her shoulder. Sarah was puzzled by Shawn's display of affection for her sister. It surprised her to see it because of what she'd overheard Shawn saying to Huzzy when she first introduced herself.

Huzzy had said, "It looks like a very fine group to be with."

Shawn had replied, "Or without."

Oh, well, Sarah thought to herself, I'm glad Annie likes her.

Sarah's thoughts were interrupted by Huzzy's authoritative voice calling out instructions for casting off. Each of the girls was assigned a job, and Huzzy patiently went over the details of their individual duties. She stood tall and looked out across the harbor. Seeing that there were more empty moorings than occupied ones, she said, "It should be easy going out today. The path is straight and clear. Are you ready to sail?"

"Oh, yes!" Libby answered excitedly for all of them.

With the mainsail luffing gently in the breeze, Huzzy lowered the centerboard, then took hold of the helm, pushing the tiller over to the leeward, away from the wind. In a single smooth motion Huzzy had the tiller where she wanted it. She looked up and checked the telltale and the sails. The mainsail shook, making a *thwap-ing* sound as the wind tried to fill it. This was Huzzy's sign that it was time to cast off the jib sheet. She called out the order to Allison and Sarah who stood ready by the smaller sail. "Cast off!"

The two girls worked quickly together. They untied and threw off the lines from the T-shaped cleats at the bow of the boat. Libby and Annie hurried to do their job. They coiled the bow lines neatly back into their sleeping snake position. Huzzy looked pleased as she saw the girls following her orders without problems.

Shawn had listened intently as Huzzy explained her duties and seemed to be a natural sailor. She caught on to everything right away. Now she was prepared to haul in the jib sheet when Huzzy called the order to her. She watched for the mainsail to fill with wind. In a minute it did, and Huzzy pointed to Shawn, "Jib sheet, Shawn!" With her long hair doing some luffing of its own, Shawn gracefully pulled in the jib sheet until the sail was well trimmed and tight against the wind.

Huzzy eased the tiller back to its midships position, and the boat moved off through the harbor and out to open sea. Huzzy faced into the wind and a satisfied smile spread over her face. This feeling of flying across the water toward her beloved islands where every wave welcomed her made her breathe deeply. The sky was clear, the ocean was smooth, and Huzzy thought of what her father always said when they sailed together under such perfect conditions. "It is your ocean, Huzzy girl, your ocean!" He said it as though he were handing the whole great thing over to her as his special gift to his special girl. Then he'd throw back his head and laugh his deep and hearty laugh, a laugh not unlike Huzzy's own.

A wave of homesickness hit Huzzy as hard as the waves hitting the hull of the *Sea Breeze*. How could these girls she was traveling with ever know the real pull of her islands? she thought. She was not much older than they were, but she felt a real difference. She'd lived on an island all her life. She'd been nourished by the fruits of the plum-purple waters around her. She'd awakened every day to the song of the Bahama banana quit as it gathered its first meal of the morning from the jambu trees outside her window. The islands were as much a part of her as her heartbeat. The wave of missing home broke as she looked back and saw no shoreline, only ocean behind them. She felt good again.

"It is your ocean, girls!" she called out to her group who were spread out around the deck, two standing, two sitting, and Allison holding her hair and heading below.

Shawn responded to Huzzy's pronouncement by throwing her arms up toward the cloudless blue sky, giving herself totally to the wind. "It *is* my ocean," she whispered to the wind. "And my sky and my freedom." Her hair was lifted from her tanned shoulders and swirled around her head. As surrounded as she was by the ocean air, she still felt she couldn't get close enough to it. She blew out, adding her own breath to the salty breeze. To be a part of the air, a part of the sky, that's what she silently wished for. To paint it, to write about it, she knew she had to feel it. When she looked over at Huzzy facing the wind in the same way, Shawn had a thought. "She doesn't just feel it, she *is* it." And for the second time that day she felt sorry that she wouldn't be sharing the cabin with her. She didn't know exactly what Huzzy had, but whatever it was, Shawn wanted it, too.

"Shawn! Put your arms down! Aren't you afraid you'll be blown overboard?" Libby looked genuinely frightened.

Shawn did put her arms down and turned a perplexed look upon the younger girl. "Blown overboard?" she said in a you-must-be-joking tone. "And if I were, would that be so terrible? I can swim." Then, feeling maybe she'd hurt Libby's feelings, she sweetened her tone and asked, "Do you swim?"

Now Libby felt embarrassed by her heroic outburst. Of course the girl wouldn't blow overboard! Libby knew she always overreacted in every situation where danger was even remotely possible. She'd been that way ever since the accident. She tried to stop herself, but her mind worked against her. If she sat watching a baseball game, her mind's eye would see a baseball coming toward her and she'd duck, even when no ball was there. If she stood on a street corner, she'd always quickly step back one step imagining a car hitting her, even when no car was in sight. And when she saw Shawn with her arms held up high and the wind swirling through her hair, she had this strange vision of Shawn being swept overboard, even though now she realized it was impossible. She was sorry she'd even looked at Shawn.

"Well? Do you?" Shawn asked.

"What?" said Libby.

"Swim."

"Of course you can swim," Sarah said sweetly. "Anyone allowed on this cruise has to be able to swim, right?"

"Well, I can swim, but I'll never be in the

Olympics or anything," Libby answered, relieved that Sarah had jumped in and saved her from being over her head in conversation with the sophisticated Shawn.

Annie looked right at her sister as she said to Libby, "Sarah will show you anything you don't know about swimming. She's a perfect swimmer, aren't you Sarah?"

Her eyes lowered modestly, and her straight blonde hair fell forward. "No, of course I'm not a perfect swimmer," Sarah said softly. Then, looking at Libby cheerfully she added, "But I'll be glad to stay close to you in the water if you're worried."

Libby looked adoringly at Sarah and again pushed away her earlier thoughts of Shawn getting caught up and tossed over by the wind. "I would feel safer," she told her.

"Well, Anniekins . . . I mean, *Annie*'s a good swimmer, too, so we'll all stay together when we go swimming." She turned toward Huzzy, who stood with both hands firmly on the steering wheel, turning it right slightly to make the tiller head the boat left. "Huzzy?" Sarah called over. "Where *will* we be swimming, off the side of the boat?"

Huzzy laughed. "That is possible, of course, but I think not. For two days we will be at sea all day, but the next day we will arrive in the Abacos. The beach on Great Guana Cay is one you won't want to miss. We will stop there and you can explore the island a little. What do you think?"

"Who lives there, Huzzy?" Shawn asked, curiously. "Are there houses and all of that?"

"Oh, much more," laughed Huzzy. "There are two grocery stores, a gift shop, and even a small beach resort."

"Sounds like a regular city," Allison said sarcastically, coming back up from below, her hair neatly fluffed again. The wind battled the dark brown curls and won the fight, leaving Allison's hair tossed and tangled. "Can we get a Big Mac there?" She snickered at her own joke.

Huzzy laughed her heartiest laugh. "Allison, before this cruise is over I hope to take just a bit of your attitude away. When you see the beauty of the Abacos perhaps you will change your thinking some. There is more to live for than hamburgers and beauty tips."

"Yeah," agreed Allison. "There are also boys."

"Will you survive, Allison?" said Shawn coolly. "No hamburgers, no hairspray, no boys? A whole week without all that?"

Allison was just as cool. "I'll manage," she said.

"The question, then, is will the boys live without *you*?" Shawn continued.

Allison didn't flinch. "It'll be tough, very tough. But *some* of them might get through the whole week."

"Girls!" said Huzzy, changing the subject. "Look to starboard!" She pointed proudly over the right side of the boat.

"Dolphins!" Libby shouted, scrambling closer to the side than she ever thought she'd dare. "Look at all of them!"

Slipping up and out of the deep green-blue water were the slick gray bodies of no less than twelve dolphins. As though on cue from a ringmaster, the diving dolphins performed an ocean circus act like none the girls had ever seen before. First, two of the great seven-foot mammals arched above the sea's surface, disappearing back into the deep just as two or three others took a turn leaping.

"It's like Sea World," Allison said enthusiastically, referring to the amusement park where trained dolphins performed for audiences.

"I think it's more that Sea World is like *this*," corrected Shawn, not taking her eyes off the school of dolphins for even a second.

Huzzy looked over at Shawn. She cocked her head to the side and squinted one eye shut as the sun hit her. "Yes," she agreed, "all the places that try to bring the ocean life to people on the land would do better to bring the people on land to the ocean life." To punctuate Huzzy's point, all twelve of the dolphins chose that exact moment to leap skyward and dive nose-down into the water. It was like the last incredible blast at a Fourth of July fireworks display when the best of the sparkling bursts blaze in the black sky. The dolphins did their finale before swimming off and out of sight of the *Sea Breeze.*

"That was incredible!" Libby exclaimed. "The way they all jumped at the same time!"

"Yes, the dolphins work well together," Huzzy said. "And so must we now. Are you not hungry, you girls?"

"I have to admit when Allison mentioned a Big Mac my stomach did growl a little," Sarah said.

"Mine, too," added Libby.

"Pizza!" said Annie. "That's what would make my stomach growl."

"What?" Huzzy asked teasingly. "You mean, no one will eat the seaweed salad I prepared especially for our first lunch together?"

"Oh, sick," groaned Allison.

"Seaweed salad?" Sarah said, gulping and trying to look brave.

"What kind of dressing?" Annie asked.

"Thousand Island, what else?" Libby said, laughing.

Hunger made the girls follow Huzzy's suggestion that while she and Shawn tended the tiller and stayed the sails, the rest of them go below and get the first-day boxed lunches provided by Windswept Sailing Cruises. Allison went first, eager to comb her hair. Sarah gath-

41

ered her sister and Libby, like a mother hen with her brood, and followed Allison below. "Lunch in five minutes!" Sarah announced to all, taking it upon herself to be in charge of the galley.

"Well done, Sarah!" Huzzy called after her.

Shawn and Huzzy were alone for the first time. "So what do you think?" Huzzy said. "Is the ocean not beautiful?"

"It is beautiful," Shawn almost whispered. "I want to paint every wave. The dolphins were so wonderful, so free."

"What do you paint?" Huzzy wanted to know. "You are an artist?"

"Well, my father and mother are artists. I mean *real* artists. I have to go a long way before I can call myself an artist. But I paint, yes. I paint what I see and what I feel."

"This must be something," Huzzy said thoughtfully, "to be able to paint your feelings. This is a real talent, one I do not have."

Shawn looked into Huzzy's flawless black face and studied it carefully before she spoke. "But you have the feelings. You *are* the feelings."

Huzzy looked back at Shawn, tipped her head in her usual thinking pose, and said, "You will like the islands, I believe. You will see. The feelings will be yours to paint."

The two stood silent then, facing the wind and watching the water change colors as they sailed first over reefs of kelp and seaweed, then a sandbar, next a coral reef, and again back to deep ocean. Shawn took a mental picture of the changing colors and suddenly marveled at how Huzzy's deep black skin matched the color of the deepest part of the ocean, a blue-black that hinted at perhaps mysterious and wonderful things hidden below the surface.

"Lunch is served!" Sarah's happy voice broke the silence. Coming up the steps and carrying red-and-white boxes with the Windswept sailboat on two sides, Sarah, Annie, and Libby brought two extra lunches to Huzzy and Shawn.

"Where is our Allison?" Huzzy asked.

"She says she isn't feeling well," Libby said. "Her stomach."

"And she also just fixed her hair all over again," Annie informed her.

All the girls laughed, but Huzzy handed over the helm to Shawn and leaned her long body down below deck. "Are you all right, Allison?" she called.

"Yeah," the girl called back. "I'm going to eat down here. My stomach feels totally upset."

"It is better to be above, then," Huzzy explained. "You will feel the motion of the boat less, and the air will help when you are feeling the seasickness."

"No, thanks," Allison said with a slight moan. "I just want to stay here. I'm not really hungry."

"Well, I'm starved!" said Annie, opening the

boxed lunch and examining the contents. Inside there was a hero sandwich with tuna fish salad, fresh tomatoes, and crisp lettuce. "Umm! Tuna fish!" Annie said, taking a hero-sized bite of the big sandwich.

"Oh, no," Sarah said softly when she saw Annie's sandwich. "I hope mine isn't tuna fish. I don't really care for fish at all."

"She hates it, is what she means," Annie added, pulling out a bag of chips, a big ripe peach, a kiwi fruit, and a big square of banana cake.

"Ham," said Sarah with relief. "Ham and cheese. Perfect."

"And I have turkey with cranberry sauce," Libby said, lifting up the thick whole wheat bread for a peek inside.

Shawn found bacon, lettuce, and tomato, which was exactly what she'd hoped for, while Huzzy ate only the fruits in her own lunchbox. All the girls, minus Allison, ate hungrily while Huzzy sang an island song with a reggae beat. The words were all about the great green turtles around the tiny Green Turtle Cay, Huzzy's island. Huzzy clapped as she sang.

See the great green turtles
Swimming in the bright blue sea
They coming to the island
They coming right to me.

See the great green turtles
See how great and green they be
They coming to the island
To Green Turtle Cay.

As her strong voice clipped the words sharp and short, her pink-palmed hands gave a backup beat that was hard to sit still for. Soon Libby, Annie, and Sarah were clapping along with Huzzy as Shawn stood swaying back and forth against the motion of the boat. The verse was repeated again, and this time all the girls joined in at the end when Huzzy sang, "They coming to the island, To Green Turtle Cay."

Down below deck, Allison lay on her bed swaying back and forth, too, but her motion went with the rocking of the boat. She groaned as waves of motion sickness washed over her. Unable to stand it another minute, she finally helped herself up off the berth, through the kitchen, and up the steps to where the rest of the group was singing and clapping. When she caught sight of Shawn swaying it was too much for her. She turned and went right back down to her bed, lay down, and went to sleep hoping to forget she was on a boat out in the middle of the ocean, on her way to a place she'd never heard of before and wished she never had.

3.
The First Night

Sarah had it all figured out. She would be in charge of the supper menu, deciding what to cook. Libby would be the salad maker, and Annie would set the table with the Windswept dishes. Allison would be part of the clean-up crew, if she got up, that was. So far she'd spent the whole day in bed moaning and groaning even in her sleep. Only Sarah and Libby felt sorry for her.

Huzzy had given her best advice about staying up on deck, but Allison had ignored her. Shawn suspected that Allison just had gotten worn out from fixing and refixing her hair and makeup so many times. Annie was sure Allison just wanted to get out of helping.

"Aren't you being a little too hard on her?" Sarah said, showing the soft side Annie had grown so sick of.

Shawn opened the refrigerator door and popped open a can of Windswept Cola. "I think this *trip* is hard on her, not us," she said in answer to Sarah's question.

"More drinks in the chilly bin," Huzzy called down cheerily as she saw Shawn holding the red-and-white cola can.

"Chilly bin?" asked Libby. "What's a chilly bin?"

"Hoh," said Huzzy. "On the islands we call it a chilly bin, but you would say 'cooler.' "

"Oh, in the cooler," Annie said, understanding Huzzy now. She turned to an insulated ice chest that sat on a counter and opened the latch. Inside were jugs of milk and two or three different kinds of juices.

"Milk, orange juice, grapefruit juice, and some other stuff, I don't know what," Annie called out, ready to take drink orders.

"Papaw juice," Huzzy called down the hatch again.

"Papaw juice?" all four girls in the galley said together.

"Papaya," Huzzy explained in mainlanders' language. "The name may be different, but it is what it is."

Throughout the day the girls had caught Huzzy's unfamiliar phrases and expressions and thrown them back for definitions and explanations. When she told a story about her two brothers, Isaac and Juba, fighting over the last piece of their Mama Selina's Cay lime pie, she ended with, "And after some four days Mama finally swallowed the grunt."

It seems Isaac and Juba weren't fighting over who would get the last piece because it was so good. The fight was about who would eat it just to make their mama feel better about ruining the pie with salt instead of sugar. Mama Selina heard them saying, "You eat it!" "No, *you* eat it!" and wouldn't speak to either boy the rest of the week. At last she "swallowed the grunt," or as Huzzy explained laughingly, she forgave them and started speaking to them again.

"Papaw juice anyone?" Annie asked, holding up a bottle of the golden juice.

As Libby worked chopping celery, green peppers, and carrots for the salad, Annie filled five glasses with the drinks of choice, and Sarah expertly prepared hamburger patties and french fries. The patties were perfectly round and all exactly the same thickness. Their perfection did not escape Annie's notice. She secretly hoped one of those perfect blonde hairs would fall into Sarah's own meat patty.

"Good job, Annie," Sarah said in her motherly way. "The table looks perfect."

"Plates, forks, knives, and spoons," Annie said flatly. "How could I go wrong?" She resented Sarah's way of trying to make her feel that even a simple job was so wonderfully done and could only be done so well by Annie.

Sarah ruffled Annie's hair, smiled, and said, "I only meant it looks nice with all the red-and-white dishes and the matching napkins."

"Oh, yes, it does," agreed Libby, adding her salad bowl filled with fresh salad to the table setting.

"Everything doesn't always have to match, does it?" Annie snapped at both of them.

Shawn backed Annie up. "No, it doesn't," she said. "Sometimes things look a little more interesting if they don't match exactly. It's a surprise to the eyes if things aren't always symmetrical."

Annie looked at Shawn and noticed a perfect example of what she meant. In one ear she had one hole pierced and a silver hoop dangled from it. But the other ear had two holes pierced. The lower one had a matching hoop, but the higher one just held a tiny silver ball. Annie had noticed that right away earlier that morning, but at the time she just thought maybe Shawn had lost the other silver ball. Now she realized it was an intentional break from tradition.

"Well, I know what you mean, Shawn," Sarah said, "but it does look cheery anyway." Sarah opened the oven to check the french fries and didn't give another thought to the conversation. The french fries were ready at exactly the same time as the hamburgers were done. "Perfect," said Sarah, happy that her first meal looked as good as it was sure to taste. "Dinner is served," she sang out to all the girls.

Allison came stumbling into the light of the kitchen, squinting her eyes to hold in some last seconds of her sleeping quarter's darkness. "Ugh!" she groaned sleepily. "Food?" Sleep had restyled her hair, flattening it on one side. Bits of black mascara clung to the skin under her eyes, and the blue eyeliner she'd worn was now smeared up the side of one temple.

"Allison, you look awful," Annie blurted out, quietly promising herself she'd never wear makeup, no matter what.

"I *feel* awful," Allison slurred, holding her stomach. "And the smell of whatever you're cooking is making me feel even worse."

"Why don't you take Huzzy's advice and go on deck and get some air," Shawn suggested. "You don't have to worry about your hair now. It can't look any worse." She casually took a swig of cola and fixed a look of innocence on the seasick girl.

"Ohmigosh!" Allison said, putting a hand to her hair and suddenly realizing it probably looked a wreck.

Shawn laughed as Allison turned and went back to her cabin to repair the damage. "Well, maybe I cured her stomach troubles," she said. "Her hair hurt worse!"

"Did I hear you say 'dinner'?" Huzzy said, coming down to join the group. "And what have we this night? Something fresh from the sea?"

"Hamburgers," Sarah said.

"A new kind of fish, maybe?" Huzzy joked. "Let us give it a try, shall we?"

The girls sat down and busily began passing ketchup, salt and pepper, pickles, and relish around. "Pass the cut-up, will you, Libby?" Huzzy said. Then seeing the blank look on Libby's face, Huzzy laughed and said, "Salad, I mean. Sorry."

All the girls laughed and Allison, who was just stepping through the doorway again, put her hand up to her hair and said, "What?"

"We weren't laughing at your hair, Allison," said Shawn, hardly able to believe how someone could be so deeply involved with her appearance.

"Oh," said Allison, taking her place next to Libby and across from Shawn. "I'm feeling a little better now I think," she said cautiously. "At least I think I can eat a little something."

"Maybe you should save your strength for cleanup," Annie said.

"We will all help this first night," Huzzy said, stopping a possible discussion before it started. "This first night on the *Sea Breeze* I wish for you all to be on deck to see how she looks in the evening. There are so many lovely things to show you, and the sunset is one of the loveliest sights on the ocean. Also we will see what tomorrow's weather will be."

"Oh, do you have a TV on this thing?" Allison asked, brightening at the thought of maybe seeing one of her favorite sitcoms instead of some silly sunset.

Huzzy laughed her hearty laugh as she shook her head. "Allison," she began with amusement, "out here you do not need television. The natural sights are better than what you find on any channel you have at home. You will see. At night the ocean is a different place. If you have not been on a boat out in the middle of the ocean at night before, prepare your eyes for some beautiful surprises. And as for the weather, the sunset can tell us what tomorrow will bring."

The girls ate Sarah's perfect hamburgers and french fries, and everyone agreed that Sarah was the perfect choice as the one to be in charge of food. Libby's "cut up" was the best anyone had ever tasted. Even Allison had a bite of it and swallowed without grimacing. In fact, the first food of her day seemed to make her feel a lot better. Not so well, however, that she was first to jump up to clear the table. That was Sarah.

"Here," said Sarah in that same motherly voice, "you girls hand the dishes to me. Annie, you can scrape the plates into the garbage."

"Save the scraps of rolls for the gullies," Huzzy said as she stood to help clear. "You will enjoy feeding them from the stern."

"She means sea gulls, don't you, Huzzy?" Libby said.

"Yes, Libby, of course. Hoh, after a week with me you will understand my strange language, or perhaps I will speak *your* strange one!" Huzzy laughed at herself and then said, "You will excuse me, girls, while I go prepare to lower the flag and turn on the mast lights. You will not forget the bread for the gullies, yes?"

When Huzzy left the small kitchen area, it should have seemed less crowded. Instead, Annie noticed a more closed-in feeling coming over her. Somehow, she thought, Huzzy's lilting island accent and her calm and sure manner managed to put space between them all even when there wasn't space to spare. Now that she had gone up on deck, the space between them narrowed.

"Watch it, Shawn!" Allison snapped as the other girl brushed against her while reaching across the table to clear away the bottles of ketchup and relish.

"I will," said Shawn without an apology.

"Sarah," Annie whined, "this isn't home, you know. I don't have to go away to scrape dishes. I could do that at home. And besides, cleanup is supposed to be Allison's and Shawn's job."

"Oh, let's just do it together," Libby said cheerfully. "We'll sing a song and that will make the work go faster. My aunt Alice always says singing whisks the work away."

"She always says *that*?" Allison said, wondering why anyone would think it important to say that even once.

Libby was already singing. She clapped and sang the song Huzzy had taught them earlier. "They coming to the island. They coming right to me," sang the girl as she worked to wipe the table clean.

"Hello, Miss Reggae U.S.A.," Annie said sarcastically.

Shawn joined Libby for the last two lines. "They coming to the island, to Green Turtle Cay," she sang clapping in unison with her.

"Coming up top, girls?" Huzzy's voice called down, once again putting the needed space between them all.

"In a second," Sarah sang out, as she folded a red-and-white dish towel over the oven door handle.

Huzzy folded the Windswept flag and slipped it neatly onto the shelf under the steering wheel. The telltale was left at the head of the mast, standing out straight, showing that a steady breeze was blowing from the southwest. Out of good habit Huzzy made a note of the wind's direction in the boat's logbook. Next, she checked the ground tackle to make sure the anchor was securely lodged on the rocky reef below. This spot, just west of Grand Bahama, was the perfect mooring place for the night. In the distance the big island was barely visible, but Huzzy's main interest was the setting sun. Like a giant teaball dipping into a pot of tea water, the big orange ball dipped toward the ocean, resting for the moment on the hazy horizon. The evening sky was a bright reddish-orange, a sign Huzzy's father had taught her to read as good weather the next day.

"My girls!" Huzzy called down to the crew below. "Come up before the sun goes down!" She couldn't let them miss the blazing finish of the day.

"It's so incredibly beautiful!" Libby gasped as she caught sight of a sky that matched her hair.

Shawn came up carrying her sketch pad and colored pencils. Without saying a word she quickly sat down on a side bench and began trying to catch the colors on paper.

Sarah, Annie, and finally Allison all came up to see the sunset. Even Allison had to admit it was every bit as beautiful as Huzzy had said it would be. "It's like a giant fireball," Allison said.

"It *is* a giant fireball," said Annie. "That's exactly what it is."

"Well, you know what I mean," Allison huffed. "Anyway, it looks nice. I'm going below. It's too windy up here."

She stopped when Huzzy said dramatically, "I

see a clear and sunny day tomorrow. No rain, no clouds. Only bright sunshine the whole day through."

"How do you know that, Huzzy?" Sarah asked.

"This is something you know very well if you live on an island. Where I live the weather can be a friend or it can be an enemy. If you know what to expect and can prepare for bad weather, there is no problem. But to be caught without warning can be dangerous. The winds blow, and the waves swell so high. It is best to pay attention to the signs the sun, the moon, and the stars give us." Huzzy looked out again at the setting sun. "You see," she continued her weather lesson, "when the sun rises in the morning with a bright orange-reddish sky, bad weather is a certainty. If the sun sets with the same kind of sky it means the weather will be good the next day. Simple, yes?"

Libby shuddered. Her mind's eye was seeing things again. At the mention of danger and winds and waves, she imagined the *Sea Breeze* rocking violently on the crest of a giant wave. The feeling passed as quickly as it had come, and Libby reassured herself by studying the sunset through Huzzy's eyes. Bright orange-reddish sky. The weather would be good the next day. "Good," said Libby aloud, but to herself.

"Well," said Allison in a snippy tone, "I'm glad the weather's going to be nice. I mean, I didn't come all the way out here to get rained on or something."

"What exactly *did* you come all the way out here for?" Shawn wanted to know.

"To get away from my mother," Allison snapped back. "Or I probably should say for her to get away from me. She made me go."

"No one made us go, right, Anniekins?" Sarah said. "We wanted to go, and they only let us because we were going together." She put her arm around her sister and didn't notice Annie stiffen.

"I'm glad I came, but I do miss my aunt Alice a lot." Libby held back the tears she felt welling up in her eyes.

"Why do you live with your aunt, Libby?" Sarah asked cautiously. "Did something happen to your mom and dad?"

Sarah had asked the question to which they were all curious to know the answer. Now all the girls looked at Libby where she sat facing the setting sun. She was silent for a minute, so Sarah was just about to apologize for asking. Then Libby told the terrible story of coming home from a school field trip to a Seminole Indian reservation. Everything had been so wonderful that whole day, she remembered. Everyone was happy to be away from school, and there had been lots of laughing and singing on the bus to and from the reservation.

When the bus pulled up to the elementary school all the mothers were waiting to pick up their children. One mother was missing. Libby's mother. Libby had stood on the sidewalk waiting and watching as one by one, each of the other classmates drove off. The teacher stayed with Libby, but finally they went inside the school office and called Libby's house.

"When I saw Mrs. Higginson's face I knew something was wrong," Libby told the girls. "She just kept saying, 'Oh, no. That can't be. Oh, no. That can't be.' " It had been a police officer who had answered the phone and had told the teacher there had been a car accident.

"My mother had driven to town to meet my dad at his office for lunch. On their way back, well" — Libby hesitated and took a deep breath — "I guess they didn't get back."

"Oh, Libby, that's the saddest story I've ever heard, ever," Sarah said, putting her arms around the girl.

"I can't believe that could really happen," Annie said. "It seems too, too unfair."

Allison didn't say anything. She only thought about how many times she might have secretly wished her mother would be gone. She had never thought it through, but hearing Libby's story made her appreciate her mother. Sort of.

Shawn stood up and came over to Libby. "Here, Libby," she said, handing her the finished sketch she'd been working on. "It's you."

"It *is* me!" Libby said, her smile coming back as she stared at the perfect penciled likeness of herself sitting against the backdrop of the fiery orange sky.

"Certainly you may call yourself an artist, Shawn Kallin," said Huzzy when she looked over Libby's shoulder. "You have captured the image of Libby, but there, too, you have the many colors of the sunset. It is very beautiful."

"Thank you," said Shawn quietly.

"And thank *you*," Libby bubbled to the artist. "This will be the best souvenir of this vacation. I'll always keep it, forever and ever."

Shawn laughed at Libby's flattering enthusiasm, although it embarrassed her a little. Coming from a family of artists, she never really felt the compliments she got were deserved. She measured her work against that of her father and mother who both showed their paintings in galleries all over the country.

"Hey, what about those gullies, or whatever you call them?" Annie said. "I thought we were going to feed them?"

"There they wait," Huzzy said, pointing to the six sea gulls that had signed on to the cruise back at the dock. They floated peacefully on the surface of the water, waiting patiently for dessert.

Sarah had piled the scraps neatly on a Windswept plate, and now she began handing out equal amounts to the girls. Shawn was the only one who said, "No thanks." She wanted to sketch a little more while there was still some light left.

By the fading light of dusk and to the sound of Huzzy's happy, "Here, gully, gully!" Shawn made her first drawing of all the girls. Five figures leaned out to the gray-and-white birds that hovered weightlessly above their outstretched hands. Each girl squealed with a little delight and a little fright as the big yellow beaks plucked the bread from their fingertips. Shawn sketched quickly and caught the gullies, the girls, and the last of the light in a dusky darkening sky. Now the only light left came from those on the mast, which swayed back and forth like a metronome ticking in three-quarter time.

As darkness draped itself around the girls, the excitement of the long first day brought yawns and sleepy stretching. No one wanted to be the first to say it, but all the girls were tired.

Allison, who had meant to go below hours before, confessed first to being worn out. "I don't know about anyone else," she said, "but I'm ready for Sack City. All this fresh air is killing me."

"I do not think it is doing quite that, Allison," Huzzy laughed. "But you are right. It is best to get settled for the night. We will have another long day of sailing tomorrow."

"At least this thing isn't rocking too much now," Allison said. "I couldn't take a whole night of that sick-to-my-stomach feeling."

"I think the rocking will put me right to sleep," Libby said, holding her special picture carefully as she followed Allison down the steps.

"Yeah, me, too," Annie said, not realizing she was agreeing with the girl she'd decided not to like as soon as she saw her.

"Well, we'll all go right to sleep then," Sarah said. "Just a quick teeth brushing, then straight to dreamland, right, Anniekins?"

Annie was too tired to remind Sarah not to call her that. "Right, Sarah," she said in the middle of a yawn.

Shawn noticed Huzzy checking all the lines on the cleats to make sure they were secure. "I'll help you do that, Huzzy," she said, laying her pad and pencils down. She watched carefully as Huzzy retied some lines that were too loose and as she once again checked the anchor line. A sudden swift wind caused Huzzy to tip her head to the side and wrinkle her brow as she obviously tried to figure out something. She checked the telltale and stayed watching it for a moment.

"What is it, Huzzy?" Shawn asked. In the hazy glow of the mast lights, she could see the perplexed look on Huzzy's face.

Huzzy quickly snapped out of her trancelike gaze at the telltale. "Oh. Nothing," she said, brushing off a strange feeling as unimportant. "Just the wind."

Shawn retied a line on a cleat near her sketching things, then picked up the pad and pencils. It was too dark to really see her drawing now. She had to wait until she was in the cabin below to examine it closely. "Well, I guess I'll go down now," she said to Huzzy.

"Yes," Huzzy replied. "I will follow shortly." When Shawn had disappeared below, Huzzy took another look at the telltale. It still stood out straight, but now it blew in a different direction. She wrote a note in the *Sea Breeze* log: *Wind out of the northeast.*

Before joining the others, Huzzy tried to focus her eyes on the distant darkness. She blinked, trying to see something, anything. Her ears strained to hear any sound that might be different or unusual. It was her ocean, but this night her ocean wasn't saying anything to her. The waves slapped the sides of the boat. The mainsail lines clinked against the aluminum mast like the chains of some wandering ghost. Huzzy leaned her body out over the black ocean. With no moon for a nightlight, the darkness seemed as thick as the dampness that settled on the boat. Her eyes made an adjustment, and Huzzy could see the gullies floating close to the boat. Their heads were tucked into their feathers for the night, but one great gray gully seemed on alert. His head turned and his round eye met Huzzy's eyes as the two both seemed on the lookout for a nightstalker.

In a minute even that one gully tucked his hooked beak under a wing and seemed to be at peace. "Not a worry in the world, eh, gully, gully?" Huzzy laughed off her own uneasiness. Then she wondered, "What might I know that the gullies don't?" But she didn't have the answer to that one.

"Huzzy?" Sarah's voice floated up through the dark.

"What is it, Sarah?" Huzzy answered.

"Libby's crying," whispered Sarah. "I can't seem to make her feel any better. I think she's homesick."

"I will be right there, tell her please," Huzzy said, looking around once more before leaving the deck in the care of the night sky. As she hurried down the steps into the galley area, Huzzy could hear Libby's quiet sobbing. She quickened her step, passing through the cabin where Sarah, Annie, Allison, and Shawn were half settled in.

"I hope she's not going to be doing that the *whole* night," Allison complained.

"You could always sleep up on deck instead," Shawn suggested.

"Oh, right," Allison snapped. "And listen to that spooky clanking all night? I don't know which is worse, crying or chains rattling."

"Shhh," Sarah said softly. "You don't want to make it worse, I'm sure."

"No," Allison said, plopping down on her bunk in exaggerated exhaustion. "I certainly don't want to make anything worse. But if I have to hear that crying all night I'll get a splitting headache."

As if on cue, a can of hair mousse rolled off her shelf right at that moment and clunked the girl on the head. "Oh!" she said, putting her hand up to the spot where a red mark was forming on her forehead.

"Are you all right?" Sarah asked worriedly right away.

Annie could hardly hold in her laughter. "Well, I hope *she's* not going to be crying all night now, too!"

They were all surprised to see that tears really were gathering in Allison's eyes even though she tried to hide them.

Sarah quickly ran into the galley and got a piece of ice. She wrapped it in a paper towel and gave it to Allison to put on her wounded spot. Annie handed the girl a tissue, then rolled over and faced the wall. Shawn got up, went into the bathroom, and shut the door on Allison's problem. She took her time washing the salty sea air off her face and brushing her bright white teeth. When she finally came back out, the other three girls were already asleep. Shawn could hear Huzzy's soft voice singing some comfort to her homesick cabin mate. It was a song Shawn had never heard before, and she knew it must be one known only to the islanders. The words and gentle tune worked to soothe Libby. Huzzy sang:

> Little girl, little girl my own
> When you be sleeping
> You dream you be home
> You dream you see your island
> Sitting in your hand
> You dream you be home soon
> On your island sand.
> Little girl, little girl my own
> Soon, so soon you be
> On your island home.

Shawn opened her sketch pad and studied the picture she'd drawn. All the girls looked right to her except Huzzy. She picked up a red-colored pencil and drew a flower in Huzzy's hair. It hadn't really been there, but Shawn knew it was the right thing to do for a girl from the islands. When she was finished, she closed her pad, turned out the light over her bed, and lay listening to the last notes of Huzzy's song. Just as she was about to sleep, she was brought back to wakefulness by a rustling sound.

In the darkness of the cabin with the even breathing of all the others, Shawn held her own breath and listened. She quickly realized the rustling was Huzzy slipping quietly through the cabins and up the steps again to the deck above. Shawn watched as the hem of Huzzy's white nightgown ascended the stairs and vanished from view. As she tried to keep her eyes open she found herself being lulled to sleep the same way that Libby was, by Huzzy's soft song.

> *You dream you be home soon*
> *On your island sand.*
> *Little girl, little girl my own.*
> *Soon, so soon you be*
> *On your island home.*

Huzzy's voice spilled into the darkness of the cabin. Soon Shawn lay sleeping just like all the other girls.

> *When you be sleeping*
> *You dream you be home.*
> *You dream you see your island . . .*

Huzzy's voice drifted off into the wind that had picked up and was causing the mainsail lines to clink and clank even louder now. The song she sang did not comfort Huzzy as it always had when her Mama Selina had sung it to her. Instead, the song made Huzzy feel wide awake, and the burden of the responsibility for these five girls, who were so different from each other, weighed heavily on her.

Following the lead of the gullies, Huzzy tucked her head under her arm. The warmth of her own breath *was* a comfort to her, and soon the soft rocking of the boat, the steady clinking of the lines, and the *whoo*ing of the ocean wind coaxed the wakefulness from her. Huzzy slept.

4.
The Storm

Long before the sun was up, Huzzy was. Out of the gray morning mist came the shrill cry of the gullies flying with an eye to their breakfast bar, the ocean. Huzzy pulled the white canvas sailbag closer around her bare shoulders and huddled deeper into her own arms. This had not been the first night she'd slept out on a boat deck and awakened to the sound of gulls. Many times her father and she had fallen asleep watching for stars to come down out of the midnight sky. For Huzzy, outside was as comfortable as inside. The chill of the morning air only brought good memories with it, memories of her father's first words every morning.

"Huzzy girl," he'd say, holding her chin in his big hand, "the morning is here to greet you. Do not keep it waiting."

She was always as eager for morning to arrive as morning was to get there. But morning was late today. The gullies knew it and Huzzy knew it. The cloud-covered gray sky was supposed to be aglow with the light of the sun inching its way up. Last night's reddish-orange sky called for a perfect day. But Huzzy knew that out on the ocean, with winds meeting from all directions, the only sure thing was that nothing was certain.

Huzzy peeked over the side of the boat down into the water. The expected deep purple had turned black. Out beyond the coral reef the usual turquoise darkened to olive-grccn. Tiny white-capped waves broke one on another causing the boat to rock quickly.

Another piercing screech from above turned Huzzy's head. "What is it, gullies?" she asked the gliding gulls as they cut a path through the thick clouds above the *Sea Breeze.*

Two birds dove at the same time for the same fish. The screeching turned to a higher pitched *"Eeee! Eeee!"* as the gulls brutally bashed each other with their beaks. The only winner was the fish that got away. The battling birds separated and flew back to the circling flock.

Huzzy shuddered even though the breeze was thick and warm now. Something about the way those gulls turned mean when it came to food gave her a strange feeling. She wanted to stop the fight, and she found a scrap of bread left from the feeding the night before. She threw it up to them and all six gulls swooped down for it. One got it and gulped it down before the others could get even a crumb. More screeching followed, and the circle broke up as the gulls each set out in search of a good fish to call his or her own.

Huzzy watched for a while until each had been successful in the hunt. For some reason she breathed a sigh of great relief when the last of the birds had finally settled down again behind the boat with a wet and wiggling fish to swallow. The choppy seas rocked them but didn't seem to shake them. All they cared about was eating, and each kept a guarded eye on the others until the last bite was gone.

"Amen. The end," Huzzy said, standing up and stashing the folded sailbag under the bench seat that had been her bed. Standing in only her short white nightgown, she felt warm and sticky from the humidity that hung around her. The telltale showed the northeast wind still blowing and with the weather being what it seemed to be, Huzzy was anxious to set sail. She hurried down below to take a quick shower in the small aluminum shower stall. Noiselessly, in the darkness of her cabin, Huzzy undressed without waking any of the others. A glance at the glowing numbers on the digital clock told her the time was 6:03, and she figured out that she could shower, dress, and set sail by 6:30 without any problem. She grabbed clothes and a towel and slipped into the bathroom where the shower was. The warm water felt good, and as she soaped up her body she thought about the warm wind that had changed directions so suddenly. What was it her father had told her about that? she wondered. But as the spray of water pelted her shoulders, she couldn't remember ever waking up to a sky like the sky this morning, so maybe her father had never told her anything about weather like today's.

The boat began rocking when she put shampoo on her hand and rubbed it into her hair. Tipping her head back to rinse the soap out, she had a sudden feeling of falling and straightened up immediately. It was just the tipping of the boat that had made her feel that way. She reached for a washcloth and a surprise lurching of the boat threw her first against one side and then the other side of the shower stall. It was difficult to keep her balance, and the narrowness of the stall made her feel trapped and anxious to just get out. She steadied herself, but the rocking continued and she hurriedly turned off the water. As soon as the noise of the shower stopped, she realized there were other noises coming from the two sleeping cabins. All the girls seemed to be talking at once, and Huzzy couldn't tell which girl was saying what. What she heard was, "What the — ?" "What's going on here?" "Why is this happening?" and finally

71

her own name being cried out in a panicky voice.

"Huzzy! Huzzy! Where are you, Huzzy?"

Huzzy quickly pulled on her clothes and opened the door. "It is all right, girls," she shouted above their excited cries as another hard lurch threw her against the cabin wall. Looking at the scene in the cabin, Huzzy saw that more than just the girls were upset. All the things on Allison's shelf had been rocked onto the bed. Allison sat up holding a different spot on her head than the one that had been hit the night before. A small trickle of blood ran between her fingers, and the girl seemed too stunned to move.

Annie sat huddled closer to Sarah than she'd ever been, holding onto her sister with one hand and the berth rail with the other. Sarah had both arms around Annie and rocked her like a baby as if her own rocking might stop the rocking of the boat.

It was Libby who had cried out for Huzzy, and the look on her face was of pure terror. Huzzy went right to her, kneeled down so that her face was right in front of Libby's, and spoke calmly but sternly. "Do not be afraid of this, Libby. This is not the worst thing you can imagine. It is just a swell, perhaps, just King Neptune giving us a bit of a ride." She cupped Libby's chin in her hand the way her own papa always did to her. Then she turned to the others. "All of you, stay calm. It is not to worry about, this rocking. When we leave this spot we will be ahead of the wind and out of its way."

She tried to make light of a situation that looked bad for the moment. Certainly the blood above Allison's right eyebrow looked bad even though the cut was small. The blankets on all the berths were strewn around the cabin floor. Things on all the shelves were tipped over or had fallen down. Shawn's neatly arranged art supplies were scattered across her shelf. Then Huzzy realized that Shawn was not in this mess.

"Where has Shawn gone to?" she asked the other girls.

Allison lifted her hand from her head and pointed up. "Up there, I think," she said. Then she saw the blood for the first time. "Yeecch!" she said with disgust at the sight of it. She jumped up to wash the blood away, but immediately fell backward as the boat tipped and rocked some more.

Huzzy reached out a hand to steady Allison. With the other hand firmly on Libby's shoulder she called out some orders. "Girls! I would like you to all get dressed, straighten up the cabins, and leave all the loose shelf items down on the beds for the time being. We will eat a good breakfast after we get going. Right now I will go up, and Shawn will help me pull up anchor and set sail. We must work quickly if we are to be in front of whatever weather threatens."

Libby winced at the word *threaten*.

"No, no, Libby," Huzzy said firmly. "We will respect the weather, but we will work with it so it will not work against us."

"Come on now, everyone," Sarah said, gathering herself and the others to start the work Huzzy had assigned them. "Let's clean up."

"Good," Huzzy said, turning to go up the steps. "Finish and come up."

When her head emerged from below, Huzzy immediately saw Shawn standing with her face into the wind that was now even stronger. Her hair blew out behind her, and her eyes were closed so she could feel the water's motion without seeing it. She showed no fear and in fact seemed to be enjoying the pitching of the boat and the whipping of the wind. "Shawn!" Huzzy called out. The girl didn't hear her. "Shawn?" Huzzy tried again. "I will need you now."

Shawn's yellow-brown eyes opened. "Oh! What is it, Huzzy? I'm sorry. I didn't hear you over the wind."

"Yes, it is stronger now, and the sky has changed," Huzzy said, noticing that the gray had turned to a lavender-purple, and the clouds looked fat and full. "I have to go below to radio for instructions."

But a few minutes later, she returned. "The radio is dead," she said fearfully. For the next ten minutes Huzzy made quick work of pulling up the anchor, raising the sails, and heading into the wind on the course she'd plotted before the trip began. With the wind blowing as hard as it was, she knew they would make better time than originally anticipated. She expected to pass Indian Cay, Windy Cay, and Mangrove Cay by early afternoon. Then, if all went well, they would reach the Little Abaco by evening. She looked up at the sky again and saw the clouds rolling in place. Very strange, she thought to herself.

"It's very beautiful, isn't it?" Shawn interrupted Huzzy's thought.

"Yes. It is. Beautiful." Huzzy felt the strength of the water as she turned the steering wheel to keep the boat on course. The pressure of the current fought against the rudder, but the sails stayed full, and the *Sea Breeze* cut through the choppy seas. As Huzzy steered the boat, the muscles in her arms tightened until they burned. It was not easy work to sail a boat on such a sea of swells.

"Check all the lines, Shawn, please," Huzzy called out over the wind. "See that they are fastened firmly. We can make this wind work for us if we have our sails and lines in order."

Shawn moved around the boat with ease. The rocking and rolling didn't throw her off balance. Gracefully she went from knot to knot, testing each line on each cleat. "All of them are secure," she yelled across to Huzzy. The skipper nodded without taking her eyes off the course straight ahead. It took all her attention and all her strength to keep the wind, which was growing stronger, on her side.

Shawn watched in awe as Huzzy held the helm firmly. She could see the difference between yesterday's sailing and today's. The ocean had been smooth, the sunlight bright, and the sky clear blue. Yesterday the sea gulls had an easy flight to keep up with the *Sea Breeze*. Now, as Shawn looked off the stern and up to the darkening sky, she could see the birds beating their wings up and down as hard and fast as they could just to keep up with the boat. One big bird stopped flapping for a second and was blown backward. For a moment Shawn thought the gull would disappear in the wake, but he wasn't a quitter. With new determination his wings carried him forward to his position with the other struggling birds. Shawn turned and looked at Huzzy again. The girl had the same look as the gull. It was a look of strong determination and the will to beat the wind. As the boat sped along, Shawn felt a kind of excitement she'd never felt before. It was the excitement of free flight, and Shawn loved the feeling.

"What's happening, Huzzy?" Libby's frightened voice called into the wind as she came up the steps. "Why is the sky so dark? Where's the sun?"

Allison was right behind her. "This wind is going to blow my head off!" she shouted as she emerged from below. "So what's the choice here? Either feel sick as a dog below or be blown away up here?"

"Here, Allison," Sarah said coming up behind her. "Why don't you wear this around your head? I don't need it." She held out a turquoise scarf.

"It'll take more than a scarf to protect you from this kind of wind. Never mind. I'm going back down. It's too rough up here." Allison turned back down the stairs and bumped into Annie who was on the way up.

"What's the matter?" Annie asked.

"Too windy," Allison yelled over the now-howling wind.

"Not for me," Annie answered as she met the wind face-to-face.

The group on deck found spots to stand and sit where they wouldn't be bounced about too much, and they talked in shouts so they could be heard over the gale.

"Why is it so rough?" Libby asked loudly.

"What?" Huzzy called back, unable to hear the girl.

Libby tried again. "Why is it so — ?" Before

her last word came out a huge wave crashed against the side of the *Sea Breeze* and washed over the deck and everyone on it.

"Look out!" Huzzy warned too late, wiping the water from her own eyes. "Hold onto something!" she yelled, tightening her own grip on the wheel.

"This is so incredible!" Shawn exclaimed, spreading out both arms to catch all the wind.

"I'm scared," Libby cried. No one could hear her. The wind grew steadily stronger and louder. The boat sailed faster than Libby thought possible. The gulls were way behind and had no hope of catching up.

Just then a loud crackling split the sky as lightning flashed in three places at the same time. Thunder boomed. Suddenly rain flooded down on the girls, soaking them to the skin in the first few seconds. The *Sea Breeze* became weightless in the waving arms of the sea as it was tossed from wave to wave, ever forward, still on course.

Huzzy moved quickly in the blinding rain. "Everyone get life jackets on!" she shouted. "Right now! Sarah, you and Annie hand out the jackets and make sure they're strapped on tightly. Get one down to Allison as well. Shawn, we must get the mainsail down and furl her straight away!"

Shawn acted quickly to untie the lines and

roll the mainsheet loosely around the boom. Even without the sails up, the *Sea Breeze* continued cutting through the waves at an uncontrolled clip. Now the feeling of free flight felt too free even to Shawn. The speed scared her, and Libby's howling competed with the wind's wailing, adding to Shawn's fear.

"Shawn!" Huzzy ordered. "Get out the anchor. We can slow her down by dragging it over the stern! The rest of you go below now. It's too dangerous up here. Go below and stay in one place. Hold tightly to your berth rails. Go below!"

The girls in their orange padded life jackets followed their leader's orders. Lunging from side to side, Sarah, Annie, and Libby clumsily made their way down the stairs to join Allison and bring her a life jacket, which she immediately put on.

"Quickly," Sarah said to the others. "Take off your wet clothes and put on dry things. Then put the life jackets back on." As she spoke, Sarah hoped the sternness of her tone hid the terrible fear she was feeling. It wasn't supposed to be this way. No one predicted a storm. No one anticipated the possibility that six girls on a boat out in the ocean would be suddenly swallowed up by an angry mixture of wind, rain, and waves.

Libby was crying as she tried unsuccessfully to undo the tangled straps of the life jacket. "Oh, I can't do it, Sarah. I can't do it!" She gave up.

79

The tears came down as heavily as the rains up on deck. Picking up a picture of her aunt Alice from the bed, Libby clung to the memory of her aunt's warm and comforting arms. "I want to go home," she cried. "I want to be safe at home."

"Allison," Sarah said, "help Libby. She needs help. I have to get Annie's jacket off and my own, too."

But another wave crashing against the side of the boat sent all the girls reeling before any of them had a chance to undo any straps. "Hold on!" Allison screamed out. "We just have to hold on. Stop crying, Libby! Stop it!"

Now Annie was screaming. The last boom of the waves hitting the boat had loosened a shriek from her throat and she couldn't stop it. Sarah stumbled over to her sister and held her tightly against her chest as her own tears fell from her blue eyes. "It's all right, Anniekins," Sarah whispered. "Everything's going to be all right." She rocked Annie until the boat rocked them apart. Amidst Libby's unstoppable wails, Annie's screams, and Allison's shouts to both of them to stop it, Sarah had a fleeting thought. It's like a movie. Things like this don't happen in real life.

But the thunder exploding, the lightning shocking the sky, and the howl of the winds were real. And as Sarah tried to reach her other arm out to the terrified Libby, she knew that the trouble they were all in was real, too. She pulled Libby to her so that the three of them huddled together as one. Another hard rocking threw Allison onto the pile. With the breath knocked out of her, she just stayed there holding onto Sarah as though she were a life raft.

Shawn found them this way when she came pouring down the stairs, her hair plastered to her cheeks by the rain and the waves that had washed over the sides of the boat. Her clothes clung to her body as though they were painted on her, and her life jacket looked waterlogged and heavy on her shoulders. "Are you all right?" she yelled out over the deafening sounds of wind and sea.

Sarah answered, "I think so. What's happening up there?" She had to shout loudly and slowly so her words could be caught by Shawn.

"Huzzy says it's the worst storm she's ever seen. There's nothing we can do except just wait for the wind to carry us where it wants to. I came down for the charts."

"Oh," wailed Libby. "I know we're all going to die. No one will ever find us. Where will the storm take us? We're all going to die. I'm so afraid! I'm so afraid!"

"Stop that, Libby," Shawn shouted fiercely. "Stop saying that! Nobody's going to die. We all have to help Huzzy now." Shawn looked at the huddled girls' tear-streaked faces. There wasn't one of them she would have chosen to be stuck with in such a situation. "Just stay where you are and take care of each other. I'll get the charts for Huzzy."

The others couldn't really hear Shawn's words because the cabin was filled with a roaring sound coming from all about the boat. Libby covered her ears to try to keep the noises out, and they all buried their faces in each other's life jackets hoping that if they couldn't see the cabin turned upside down, perhaps it wouldn't be true.

"It's a nightmare," Allison cried out. And in fact her face had a strange, nightmarish look to it with her eye makeup smeared down both cheeks and her lipstick missing her mouth completely. The blood on her forehead had dried to a crusty maroon.

Shawn grabbed the charts from the cabinet in the forward sleeping quarters and made her way back through the kitchen and up the stairs. She looked back one more time and saw Sarah pulling everyone closer, but the screams and cries that came from that cabin told her that no amount of closeness would comfort them now. The storm was the only one in control.

"Here, Huzzy!" Shawn's mouth said, but her words were lost in a whirlpool of wind and rain. She held the charts close to her body so the wind wouldn't take them. The rocking had grown fiercer, but Huzzy held tightly to the helm, squinting her eyes and trying to see ahead through the thick blanket of rain. Through all of this Shawn could see that Huzzy was still fighting for control. She had not given in yet. Like the strongest of the gullies, Huzzy still beat her wings hard and fast. She would not be blown backward, of this Shawn was sure.

"Perhaps you'd better go below with the others," shouted Huzzy over the raging storm.

"No!" Shawn called back, taking in a mouthful of water when she did. "I want to stay with you!" As she said this another whale-sized wave reached into the boat and wrapped around Shawn, pulling her with it on its way back out. Huzzy had no choice. She let go of the steering wheel and threw both arms around Shawn, holding her with all her might. Her fingers closed over Shawn's slippery wet skin but slowly they lost their grip. Just as Shawn was about to be swept over the side, still another wave crashed against her pushing her back into Huzzy's arms.

Breathless and with her heart pounding, Shawn collapsed on the deck and lay heaving, facedown, with her arms spread out and her hands gripping the rough deck. Huzzy turned back to the wheel and saw it spinning like a roulette wheel gone wild. She clamped it between both hands and pulled on it trying to get it steady again. The current pushed hard against her efforts and, as the water from the skies and the ocean fell over her, Huzzy felt a sudden easing of the wheel in her hand. The pressure was gone. Her worst fears had come true. The rudder had snapped, leaving the *Sea Breeze* at the mercy of the storm's whim. Without the rudder there was no way to keep the boat from sliding sideways across the sea. The charts would tell her nothing. Only the wind and the ocean would know the course of the *Sea Breeze* now.

Down below, the girls felt the sudden loss of control as the rocking that made them all feel so sick worsened and changed to a spinning feeling. The darkness in the cabin matched that of the sky outside. The digital clock glowed 1:47. The storm had taken away the morning and was already swallowing the afternoon hours as well. In a wet heap, Sarah, Allison, Libby, and Annie finally let their screams turn to low sobs. One by one they let exhaustion take the screams from them. All the rocking, all the thundering, all the crashing of waves against all sides of the *Sea Breeze* could not break them apart.

Even on deck, where the noise was fiercest, Shawn lay still and silent as exhaustion held her down and kept her flattened until she slept. Huzzy still stood, holding a wheel that steered nothing. "Adrift," she said to the sea. "And where will you take us now?" she wondered with

84

her first feeling of helplessness. The movement of the boat was so violent, it seemed safer to Huzzy just to find a sheltered space on deck where she could hold onto something. She sat down by Shawn with her head still up and her eyes still staring ahead into the purple daytime darkness that stretched for miles. There was nothing for her to do now but watch and try to recognize any points of land they might pass.

Huzzy wiped her eyes. The salt water made her eyes sting, but she had to keep watching. The boat moved with the speed of the wind as the lines rattled wildly against the mast. To her surprise Huzzy could make out a silhouette of an island she knew. It seemed impossible that they had drifted so far so fast, but there was no mistaking the shape of Mangrove Cay. She and her father had sailed by it so many times. She rubbed her eyes again and watched as the tiny island disappeared off to the starboard side.

This is where the *Sea Breeze* should have turned. Huzzy knew this without looking at the course set on her charts. It was out of her power now, she knew that, too. Instead of following the natural line of small islands, the *Sea Breeze* sailed straight. Huzzy braced herself for what she knew would come. Her father had told her why they should never go straight at this point. The coral reefs grew wider, the ocean's depth grew shallower. All the charts warned the sailor that these waters were unreliable and should be avoided.

For all these hours the power of the storm had only grown. It was a storm like no storm Huzzy had ever seen or even heard of in legends of the islands. Her eyes wouldn't stop stinging. The salt seemed to burn into her eyelids, and the only relief came when she closed them for a few seconds. She did that, then jerked her head up suddenly because she realized sleep was after her. She peered into the darkness and could not tell if night had come. This whole day had been spent in darkness. What would it matter if her eyes closed? she wondered. Darkness is darkness. The stinging of the salt was too much for Huzzy. Finally she closed her eyes and let the exhaustion that had overcome the others take her as well.

Six girls were adrift, cradled in the rocky arms of the sea, and they did not feel it when the crashing of the waves against the bow of the boat turned to the bow of the boat crashing against solid rock.

5.
Chilas Cay

The screeching that stirred Huzzy and Shawn was not that of gullies. It came from below, and in the early darkness of a new morning the girls on deck did not immediately understand the reason for the noise. The wind had stopped. The rain no longer beat down on them. Shawn slowly pushed her body up and lifted her head to get a better sense of where the ear-piercing sound was coming from. She looked over to the other body now sprawled facedown on the deck and saw Huzzy begin to move.

"Aaahh!" gasped the skipper of the *Sea Breeze* as her breath was taken by a sharp pain in her ankle. She couldn't move one foot because it was trapped under the heavy boom that had fallen on her the night before. She had struggled to move it, but finding it was too heavy, she had at last fallen back into an uneasy sleep.

Shawn tried to see the problem, but couldn't find it through the morning fog that hung heavy.

Tears blurred her vision as she began to realize what had happened. Now the sounds from below grew louder in her ears, and it was crying mixed with screaming as each of the girls discovered the same thing Shawn had. The *Sea Breeze* was no longer adrift on an angry ocean. Now it was trapped between coral and rock, and both had reached sharp, jagged fingers through the fiberglass sides of the boat, tearing it apart. Seawater washed through the holes, filling the forward sleeping quarters. The boat was held high at the stern by the rocky ledge that had stopped it from drifting further.

In the cabin Allison was first to notice that the motion of the boat had changed from the rough rocking to a strangely comforting swaying. For the first time since she'd stepped onto the boat, her stomach didn't feel sick. She blinked her eyes in the darkness of the cabin and for a moment she wondered angrily why everyone had to be piled onto her bed. It was with annoyance that she pushed against whomever it was that was crushing her hand. She felt fat, but quickly realized it was only the padding of the life jacket that made her feel that way. She touched her hair and felt that it was matted and tangled as it had never been before. Suddenly a small cry escaped from her lips as her memory returned and brought back the screams and cries of the stormy night. How long ago had that been? she wondered. It was still dark, and the dampness of the night before had turned into a pool of water that Allison felt when she started to put one foot down. Another cry slipped out and this cry awakened Libby, whose wailing began where it had left off before sleep stopped it. Even in an exhausted stupor her terror had continued as her thoughts tossed her as violently as did the ocean waves.

Allison didn't tell Libby to stop crying this time. She just covered her ears and rocked herself back and forth as her own tears, black with mascara, fell down her already makeup-smeared face. In a whisper her voice cried, "What's happening here? What's happening?" And as she cried softly, a startling thought screamed in her head, "I want my mother! I want my mother!"

A hand reached out and touched Allison. "Are we all right?" Sarah's voice came from the darkness.

Three hands reached back to Sarah and held tightly to her arm. "Is it over?" Annie cried, her tears pouring out and sobs following. "Hold me, Sarah!"

Libby's hand gripped Sarah's arm, and even in the now semidarkness the other girls could see Libby's mouth wide open in a scream, but no sound came out.

"Sshhh," Sarah said, trying hard not to let her

own terror come out. There were enough cries and screams already. "Sshhh," she said again. "We're all right. Everything's going to be all right. We're all right." She began to untangle herself from the pile, but Libby and Annie both clung to her, pulling her down. She stayed a minute, putting a mothering hand on Annie's head. "It's all right. It's all right, Anniekins," Sarah said over and over, hoping if she said it often enough it would be true. The false calm in her voice worked to comfort Libby, too.

Shawn's voice broke through the muted crying. "Is everyone all right?" she asked, her own voice cracking as her eyes tried to adjust to the cabin's dim light. From behind her the first rays of sunlight crept into the dark space. "Is anyone down here hurt?"

"Where are we?" Allison managed to ask.

"Is the storm over?" Libby said between sobs.

"The storm is over," Shawn said. "But Huzzy is hurt. I need — "

"Hurt!" Allison cried out. "Is she dead? How will we keep going?"

"Stop it!" shouted Shawn. "All of you, stop it! I need you to help me, and we have to get off this boat. The water is coming in, and I don't know how long it will stay afloat."

"I knew something terrible would happen to us," Libby wailed.

"Come along now, Libby," Sarah said firmly

but kindly. "Huzzy needs us. She needs all of us now."

Sarah and Allison untangled themselves first and stepped down onto the floor. "Ugh!" said Allison as her shoes filled up with water. It came over her ankles and as she moved the other foot down, the boat moved slightly forward, causing even more water to come rushing over her legs.

"Careful!" warned Sarah. "Move slowly."

The cries of the younger girls didn't stop them from moving off the bed and onto the water-filled floor, too. Libby turned to find the picture of her aunt Alice, but it wasn't anywhere in sight. She moved one foot forward and a sharp edge hit against her shin. She bent down and picked up the floating object. It was the picture, still smiling out at Libby even though the water had drenched it. She clasped it to her and moved forward toward the steps where the others were headed. Somewhere in her mind she heard her aunt's voice softly saying, "As long as you have fear keeping you a prisoner, you'll never be free." Well, she thought, I am not free yet. I'll never be free. A whimper came from her, but she kept moving.

As the girls waded through the water that had come into the *Sea Breeze*, the fear they felt mingled with hope as they all saw the rays of sunlight growing wider and wider. It was a welcome sight to come out of the darkness of the watery cabin and see the sky ablaze with the rising sun they'd expected to see the morning before.

Libby gasped. "The sun!"

A soft moan came from the stern. "Shawn?" Huzzy said in a controlled voice. "I believe my ankle is badly hurt. You and Allison and Sarah will need to work together to lift the boom off my leg."

The girls could hear the pain in their leader's voice, but she wasn't giving in to it. "Don't worry, Huzzy," Sarah said, moving cautiously through the sails and tangled lines that blocked the path to where Huzzy lay pinned under the boom and rigging. "We can do it."

Allison saw Huzzy sprawled out and trapped, and she suddenly felt trapped, too. If Huzzy could get hurt any of them could, she thought to herself. She put her hand up to the cut on her head and winced as though the pain were fresh. Huzzy winced at the same time. "You must help me now," she said, looking right at Allison.

Allison looked back at Huzzy for a split second and was struck by the thought of how much they all needed her. She stopped thinking of her head and moved around the heavy boom and helped Shawn and Sarah lift it and move it aside. They worked in a terrified trance, trying to clear away the mess the storm had made, and pull Huzzy out from under the boom. While the three older girls tried to concentrate on freeing Huzzy,

Annie and Libby stood amidst the fallen sails watching helplessly. Seeing their leader struck down was too much for the girls, and for Libby it was a terrible reminder of another accident. When at last Huzzy was freed, she attempted to stand but failed. Her ankle was so swollen it couldn't take any weight at all. She clenched her teeth together as if to hold in the pain as she fell against the bench seat, causing the *Sea Breeze* to tip slightly.

Libby screamed as she felt the boat move and heard the sloshing of more water rushing into the cabin through the gaping hole in the side of the boat. "Huzzy! We're sinking!" She pulled at her red hair and looked around for a safer place to stand.

"It is all right, Libby," Huzzy said as calmly as she could. "Girls, we will have to leave the boat."

"Leave!" Allison exploded. "Leave for where?"

"For there," Shawn said, pointing to what she now noticed for the first time. As the sun rose higher in the sky, the fog burned off leaving a thin film of haze. Through it the girls could see a white sand beach meeting the turquoise water that innocently lapped the shoreline. "It's an island," she said. "We're on an island!"

"What island?" Annie asked hopefully. "Do you know, Huzzy?"

Libby brightened. "Is it your island, Huzzy?"

she asked, a smile almost coming to her mouth.

"No. It is not Green Turtle," Huzzy said, rubbing her swollen ankle.

Both Annie and Libby immediately felt tears welling up in their eyes all over again. Sarah noticed that the swelling of Huzzy's ankle was getting worse now that she sat upright. The girls' tears would have to wait, she thought. "We have to do something about your foot, Huzzy," she said.

"Yes. I am afraid I will not be much help if I cannot walk. Shawn, please get the oars from under the seat on the other side. Move carefully, and you others stay as you are. I do not know how long the coral reef will hold us."

Shawn followed Huzzy's instructions, and together she and Sarah made a makeshift crutch out of the oars and a short paddle. Now Huzzy was able to stand and resume her role as leader. Seeing her up again made all the girls feel a little relieved. It was good to hear her calling out orders the way she had done before the storm, and they were more than willing to take direction from her. Fear made them work fast to beat the tide that was coming in around them. Water filled the cabin at a pace just slow enough to allow them to form a human chain leading from the forward storage area, through the two sleeping cabins, the galley, and up the stairs.

With Shawn at the storage end passing food, water, and supplies to Sarah, who passed them to Allison, who passed them to Annie, and finally Libby, who piled things on deck, the girls were able to empty the lower quarters of everything. The plan was to remove every scrap of food, every blanket, every dish, candle, cooking utensil, and whatever else they could. With each object they passed along the chain, the girls got a clearer understanding of what was happening. Their boat had crashed. They were removing everything from it. They would not be going back on it again. They were going to be stranded on this island, and they didn't know for how long.

By the time they were finished, the inside of the boat had been stripped completely, and the deck was piled high with things to be moved onto the island. They didn't finish a minute too soon. With the cabins emptied out, the weight shifted and the boat tipped, allowing the water below to flow up the stairs.

Libby saw it first. "We're sinking!" she shrieked. "I know we're sinking!"

No one argued with her. "Yes," agreed Huzzy. "The *Sea Breeze* will not last much longer. We must take as much as we can ashore." She saw the looks of shock and fear on the faces of Allison, Sarah, Libby, and Annie, so she turned to

Shawn. "You must go into the water first. It is not deep here. You will help the others off the boat."

"Not *into* the water!" Libby cried.

"Into the *water?*" Annie asked, feeling as afraid as Libby sounded.

"We must leave the boat," Huzzy said again firmly. "I will remain on board to hand things over. Form the same chain to the sand. Annie, you and Libby will stand on the sand and in the shallowest part. But you must put your tears aside and do this *now*."

Huzzy didn't mean to sound so tough, but she saw that what Libby said was true. Her boat was sinking. She looked around at the wreckage on the deck and felt a pain in her heart worse than the one in her ankle. As she looked at the girls she remembered what John the van driver had said. "I'm sure you'll make sailors of them in no time." And now there was no time.

"Hurry now, girls," Huzzy ordered. "The time is running out."

Shawn easily jumped over the side and declared the water to be like a bath. The fish at her feet didn't bother her a bit, but when Annie climbed down and felt the tickling tail of one she ran to shore. Libby climbed over next and followed Annie without waiting to feel anything. Sarah and Allison joined Shawn in the water and formed the chain from the boat to the shore.

It took hours to complete the task, but at last the *Sea Breeze* stood empty and bare. Shawn, Allison, and Sarah all helped Huzzy over the side and into the water, and Annie and Libby stood on shore. As Huzzy left the boat, the weight of it shifted again and with a great crashing sound the *Sea Breeze* slipped out of the grasp of the rock and reef, sinking bow-first into the warm waters.

Libby cried out. "No!"

Annie covered her ears to keep out the sound of the truth, but didn't take her eyes off their home-away-from-home as it sank beneath the surface of the water. "It's gone!" she gasped.

Allison, Shawn, Sarah, and Huzzy stopped where they were, waist-deep in the water, and watched the boat make its final descent. All they saw were the bright red letters that spelled out her name, blurred by the clear blue water that had swallowed *Sea Breeze* whole right before their eyes.

"Yes," said Huzzy softly and sadly. "She is gone." Then as quickly as the *Sea Breeze* had sunk, Huzzy raised her own head, looked around at her girls and added, "She is gone, but we are here. And this is what we must be thankful for now."

The girls on shore moved into the water. Those in the water didn't move at all. With the *Sea Breeze* gone all of them seemed to realize at once that the island was the only place they could go now. But for the moment the water seemed less frightening than an island about which they knew nothing. The sun beating down directly overhead forced them to finally make a choice.

"Shall we go ashore then?" Huzzy decided for them. Leaning on Shawn and the crutch, Huzzy led the way and the others followed until they reached the piles of supplies and other things carried from the boat. Exhausted from crying and all the lifting and carrying, the girls collapsed on the sand, out of strength, out of tears, and out of words for the moment.

It was Sarah who first mentioned food. They had not eaten since the night before the storm, and once she reminded them of that fact they all felt starved. All her life Sarah had found the best way to deal with problems was to just keep busy, and she did that now. She sorted through the supplies and began to put together sandwiches for everyone.

Huzzy stopped her. "Until we know what food we can find on the island we must only eat as much as we absolutely need to keep up our strength. We do not know how long we must make these supplies last."

"Oh, of course," Sarah said, putting back the cheese and lettuce, leaving only sliced turkey out.

"Well, wait just a minute here," Allison sputtered. "You don't mean someone isn't going to come and take us out of here, do you? I mean they're not going to just leave us stuck out here in the middle of nowhere!" She shook her head with the same gesture of annoyance her mother used whenever Allison interrupted her phone life.

Shawn was already turning her head in every direction, letting her eyes take in the brightness of the sand, the sparkling clarity of the turquoise ocean, the healthy green of the tall trees that all leaned in the same direction. It was the most beautiful place she'd ever seen. The palette of colors had been perfectly selected, from the azure-blue of the sky, to the purpley-gray of the volcanic rock shoreline. She only half heard Allison, but her answer was automatic. "This is not nowhere," she said dreamily. "This is some-place between heaven and paradise. I'm sure of that."

Allison just glared at Shawn. The other girls gave her a bewildered look. None of them felt ready to just sit back and enjoy the scenery. While Shawn saw the island beauty Huzzy had described so well, the others looked away from the island to the vast stretch of ocean that meant nothing to them except a memory of a terror-filled night that had ended with them all being lost.

As they lay draped over suitcases and boat

cushions, the discomfort of the wet clothes and gritty sand all over their sunburned arms and legs made them feel as washed up as the seaweed on the sand next to them. The thin sandwiches prepared by Sarah brought them back to life. Huzzy cocked her head to the side as she watched the girls hungrily tear into the bread and turkey. As they ate, they hunched over the food as if to protect it from some unseen thieving hand. Eyes darted left and right as each girl silently pulled at the food and quickly swallowed each bite. The memory of the gullies fighting over the single crust of bread the morning before sent a chill through Huzzy's sun-drenched body. The gullies and the girls did not look so different to her now.

When the last crumb was devoured, Sarah passed around a single can of Windswept Cola for all of them to share. Libby took the first sip and passed it to Annie. Annie then passed it to Shawn who handed it over to Allison. The others watched as Allison gulped instead of sipped the soda. "Allison!" Sarah scolded.

"What?" said the girl innocently. "I was thirsty."

"We're all thirsty," Annie said.

"She should be punished," Shawn said coolly.

Huzzy spoke calmly. "Allison, this must be a lesson for you. We cannot do what you have just done. We do not know yet if there is fresh water on this island. Some of the islands do have it. Some of them do not. Until we find this out, we must take care to make the water and other drinks last. And we must all be equal here. There can be no special privileges."

"Sorry," Allison growled, handing the can over to Huzzy. "Nobody told me the rules in Nowhere Land."

"I do not think we are nowhere," Huzzy replied. "If one of you could find the charts for me I believe I may be able to figure out where we have landed."

Annie jumped up and began searching through the pile of things. She pushed aside cushions, sailbags, and the life jackets they'd laid out to dry in the sun.

"Here they are!" she cried out, holding up the plastic laminated nautical charts. "Right where they belong, of course, here with the pots and pans and Allison's makeup." She handed the charts to Huzzy.

"You found my makeup!" Allison said, not hiding her joy at the discovery.

"Oh, Allison," Shawn said with disgust. "Makeup? Here?"

"Yes," Huzzy said, examining the charts closely. "Right here." She was pointing to a spot where only water was shown.

"Where?" asked Sarah, moving closer to Huzzy. "I don't see any island there."

All the girls gathered around their leader, being careful not to bump against her damaged ankle. "There's nothing there," Libby said.

"No, Libby," Huzzy disagreed. "Something is there. *We* are. If my calculations are correct and it was Mangrove Cay we sailed past last night, I believe we are in this area." She pointed to a place just slightly west of Mangrove Cay. On the chart there was a printed note saying that the area Huzzy pointed to had many uncharted cays, shallow waters, and wide coral reefs.

"But if this island isn't on the chart, does that mean no one knows it's here?" Annie asked intelligently.

"Oh that's just great," Allison said sarcastically, the pitch of her voice getting higher. "Six girls go out for a little boat ride and end up lost forever on some island no one ever heard of!"

"Don't say that, Allison!" Libby shouted, new tears flooding her eyes.

Sarah looked worried, too. "Is that true, Huzzy?" she asked, looking over at Annie to see her reaction to this.

Annie chewed her fingernail and kept her eyes on Huzzy, waiting to hear what she had to say. "Is it?" she asked.

Huzzy was silent and thoughtful before answering. She looked around at the sandy, sunburned faces of the group for which Windswept Sailing Cruises had felt she was capable of being responsible. It had been her job to make sure all the girls were kept safe going to and from the islands. Looking down at the chart again, she wondered for how long she could keep them safe on this island? It was one no boat would be passing by. She was sure of that, but what good would it do to give this information to girls who were already too frightened? She looked out to the reef where the *Sea Breeze* had gone down. What would her father have said now? she wondered. He would have known what to tell these girls who looked to her for leadership the same way Huzzy looked to her father.

Huzzy turned her eyes back to the island and saw the tall casuarina trees bending in a frozen pose all in the same direction. She felt a breeze on her face, the same breeze that blew the trees but didn't move them back to an upright stance. Then she remembered a story her father had told her many times. It was a story his father had told him many times as well.

Looking from worried face to worried face, Huzzy began. "I think we are not on an island no one has ever heard of," she said with certainty. "Many have heard of the tiny island somewhere between Mangrove and Green Turtle. Years ago another storm carried another boat to the same rocky shore. It was a ship called *Kayaska*, and the captain was a Greek sailor by the name of Chilas. He washed up on the shore just as we have, and spent every day working to build a boat to carry him to some civilized island. After more than a year this Captain Chilas finished his boat and sailed to Green Turtle Cay." Huzzy paused and looked at her listeners who were completely attentive.

"More than a year? You've got to be kidding!" Allison said, horrified.

At this point in the story Huzzy knew what her father always said. "Huzzy," he would say seriously, "this man had great courage. Though his hands bled from the coarseness of the sisal plants he wound into ropes to hold his boat together, he did not give up. Every day he waited by the shore for another board from his sunken ship to wash ashore. And every day he added one more board to his means of escape."

Huzzy continued the story. "This man had great courage," she said, and she went on to say word for word what her father had always told her. "And every day he added one more board to his means of escape." She finished with the same message her father gave to her. "So we must realize the importance of taking any problem one board at a time. If we look for the whole solution at once it may seem too great a task. But one board at a time is never impossible."

"Is this island *that* island?" Libby asked suspiciously.

"Chilas Cay the island came to be called, and

it was never put on the charts because Captain Dimitrios Chilas was the only one known to have ever set foot on it. The waters are too shallow in this area, and the reefs are too jagged. To my eyes, this island matches that of the legend, and our course directed by the storm certainly led us to the spot where Chilas Cay has always been known to be," Huzzy explained.

"So the good news is somebody has heard of it, and so they'll be along any minute now to take us off this Nowhere Cay, right?" Allison asked.

"Chilas Cay," Libby corrected, feeling a little better for their resting spot to have a real name. "It's a true story, isn't it, Huzzy?" Her tear-streaked face looked trusting and hopeful.

"Oh, yes, Libby. Very true. It is a story everybody on my island knows." Huzzy adjusted her swollen ankle and bravely ignored the throbbing pain.

"Why would he have wanted to leave such a beautiful place as this?" Shawn asked, standing to let the warm breeze cool her off a little. To her this was the kind of place her father would have painted. It was a place where her life could be filled with surprises. She shielded her eyes from the bright sunlight and looked around for some shade.

Huzzy knew what Shawn was looking for. "Back by the tree line," she said. "It is there that we must move all of our things. We must get the food out of the hot sun, and then to set up shelter for the night is our next job."

Libby turned white under her freckles. "Night? You mean we're going to sleep here tonight?" It didn't seem possible that more tears could flow from her eyes, but Huzzy's face became a blur.

Shawn laughed. The others didn't. They hadn't really thought about nighttime. Huzzy saw fear taking over again and tried to stop it. "It is true that we must stay here this night, but one night I think we will be able to get through. Then tomorrow when the day is new we shall watch for rescuers that are sure to come." For the first time small smiles peeked through the clouded looks of worry on the girls' faces. Huzzy kept the mood going by trying to sound cheerful. "It is too hot right now to be moving things. Why don't you have a swim first?"

Sarah saw what Huzzy was trying to do, exactly what she would do, keep them all busy. "Yes! Come on, Anniekins. You, too, Libby. Let's all go."

"Oh, I don't think I . . ." Libby began, her tears not yet dried.

With a sudden urgency Sarah seemed determined to make everyone swim. "Yes," she said again, "we'll all swim now." She started rummaging wildly through the piles of clothes they'd carried off the boat, looking for bathing suits. She roughly threw things aside until she'd found what she was looking for. Quickly they changed and felt glad to get out of the soggy, sandy clothes they'd been wearing since the day before. While Huzzy sat propped up against a pile of suitcases watching the girls trying to have some fun in the water, she thought about the night ahead. Was she wrong to have given them some hope about rescuers coming? She didn't really know, but with no boat to carry them home, hope was all she could offer to at least carry them through the night.

For the next hour the girls ran in and out of the water like sandpipers daring the waves to catch them. Libby stayed close to Sarah. Annie swam alone, then sat at the water's edge watching Shawn swim too far out. Allison treated the ocean like her own personal bathtub, dabbing the water over her body to wash away the sand and stickiness of dried salt on her skin. She washed away the streaks of black and blue from melted eye makeup, and to the surprise of the others, Allison looked a lot younger.

And softer, Sarah thought. She doesn't look so tough and cold.

"OK, you guys. Quit gawking at me. I wasn't born wearing makeup, you know," said Allison when she caught Sarah, Annie, and Libby staring at her.

"You look great!" Annie blurted out before she could catch herself.

"Yeah, right," Allison sneered. For years her mother had been telling her how a little blush would really help, or a dab of mascara would change her life. Even when photographs of Allison were taken when she was little, her mother always penciled in extra eyelashes and lengthened the ones already there.

"Why settle for less when more is so easy to have?" her mother always said.

"Really, Allison," Sarah agreed with her sister. "You don't even need makeup."

"Everyone needs makeup," Allison's mother always said.

"Everyone needs makeup," Allison repeated to Sarah.

What everyone really had needed was the swim, but once they'd allowed themselves the break from reality, Huzzy had to bring them back. "Girls!" she called out from where she now stood leaning on the crutch made from the oar. She motioned with her left arm for them to come back onto the beach. Sarah led Annie and Libby over to Huzzy. Allison spent a few more minutes wringing the water out of her hair and trying to fluff it dry with her hands. Shawn started the long swim back to shore when she saw the others walking in. She was the last to join the group that was gathered around Huzzy.

Shawn said, shaking the water from her hair, "That ocean is just too beautiful. I could have kept swimming for miles."

"It is beautiful today," Huzzy agreed. "Certainly we can feel more friendly toward it now than yesterday. But we must forget the ocean right now and make our camp. We still have plenty of daylight left to work in."

"Where will we make this camp, Huzzy?" Libby asked worriedly.

"Camp!" Allison said, horrified. "The last thing I wanted to do was go camping! How will we cook? Where will we sleep?"

"Where will you plug in your hair dryer?" Annie added, pretending innocence. But her joke only served to remind them all that this was not home and was not even close to home.

Seeing the sudden sadness starting to spread over her sister's face again, Sarah tried being practical. "Somehow in *Swiss Family Robinson* they figured out a way to make everything they needed," Sarah said practically. "And so will we."

"And it's only for one night, right, Huzzy?" Libby reminded them.

Shawn spoke before Huzzy had a chance to answer. "Well, you girls can stand here and discuss things if you want to, but I want to get this stuff up to the tree line and then start exploring the island a little." She picked up an armload of supplies from the pile and started to walk.

"Yes," said Huzzy, "I, too, would like to see what help we can expect from the island." She didn't finish her thought out loud, but she knew it was important to look for fresh water and fruit-bearing trees before they really needed them. "I am afraid I will not be of much help carrying things to the brush where we should set up shelters, but I am able to identify what we can eat. We shall go walking in the woods."

Libby looked frightened again. "I'm afraid of snakes," she said, her mind already crawling with unknown species of slithering snakes.

"This is one worry you do not need to have, Libby," Huzzy explained. "There are few snakes in the Abacos. You may find a lizard looking your way, but the only snakes are harmless Bahama boa snakes, and in my life I have not seen one."

"Lizards?" Libby said.

Annie shuddered. "Yeecch!" she said with disgust.

"Right now we must move our things, yes?" Huzzy said, turning the subject back to the task at hand.

"Well, what's the point of moving it all up there just so we can carry it all back down when the rescue boat comes?" Allison asked.

Again, Huzzy didn't say what she was thinking. There was no use upsetting the girls right now with the information she was sure was right. Only an accident would bring another boat to this island. "It is better, I think, to keep our things out of the sun," was all she said.

Without any more questions, the girls began carrying the piles of supplies and clothes to a natural clearing Huzzy had selected where the tree line met the sand. Under different circumstances the girls might have seen the area as beautiful. It was in the midst of some scrubby palmetto trees topped by big clusters of fanlike leaves that offered a roof over the piles of belongings. Mixed in with the palmettos were other trees with round, leathery leaves. "Sea grapes," Huzzy told the girls, pointing out the thick bunches of green grapes that hung within easy picking height.

"Can we eat them?" Sarah asked.

"We're not *that* desperate," Allison said, clicking her tongue against the roof of her mouth.

"Island people make jelly from the sea grape. They are quite tart," Huzzy explained. To herself she thought, But we may feel lucky to have them at our doorstep sometime.

"The islands have many fruits that are sweet and good to eat," Huzzy said aloud. "Figs, coco plums, wild dillies, tele-berries, wild cherries."

"You're doing it again," Libby said, grinning. "Wild dillies? Tele-berries?"

"And papaws, of course," Huzzy grinned back.

"Well, let's hope we don't *have* to eat any of that stuff," Allison said, her eyes on the ocean looking for a rescue boat.

Having finished the moving job, Shawn was ready to explore a little. "Are you all coming?" she asked, hoping some of them would say no.

The thought of lizards and even one kind of snake made Annie and Libby turn down the invitation. "No, thanks," Annie said definitely.

"I'd rather just stay here and wait," Libby added.

"I'll stay with them," Sarah volunteered.

"I'm staying here, too," Allison said. "I don't want to miss any boat going by."

"As you wish," Huzzy said. "I will go with you then, Shawn, and together we shall see what we shall see."

Shawn couldn't have been more pleased. Now she and Huzzy could explore the island without all the tears and fears of the others following every step of the way.

"You will be all right for an hour or so?" Huzzy asked, looking at Libby.

"Of course we will," Sarah said positively. "We'll just unpack."

"What!" Allison cried. "What for? Just so we can pack it all up again when they come for us? I'm just taking out what I need."

"Your mirror is right on top of the pile," Shawn said, looking directly at Allison.

"Shall we go then?" Huzzy said to Shawn, adjusting her crutch and deliberately ignoring the pain in her swollen ankle.

Shawn picked up a small canvas bag that held a sketch pad and pencils, slung it over her shoulder, and offered her other arm to Huzzy. "How will you be able to walk very far like that?" she asked.

Looking at the girls and thinking again of the responsibility she had for them her answer was direct. "I will do it because I must do it. Today we will just see if fresh water is here for us. We have a supply of it from the boat and we have a small amount of what we need to purify the salt water, but it would be better to know we will have more if we need it."

Shawn could tell that Huzzy was thinking more than she was saying. "Huzzy?" she asked. "Will a boat come?"

Huzzy looked into Shawn's yellow-brown eyes and answered her honestly. "I do not know, Shawn. I do not know."

Shawn didn't ask any more questions that Huzzy couldn't answer. The two explorers carefully made their way through the fanlike leaves and headed deeper into the thicket. It was not like an overgrown jungle. The trees seemed to grow with an easy pathway leading through them. A floor of fallen palmetto branches made walking with her crutch not too difficult for

113

Huzzy. After a few minutes Shawn stopped worrying about Huzzy, who seemed to be managing well, and began seeing only her surroundings. Ferns spread before them, opening the way to hundreds of other plants Shawn had never seen before. To her excited questions, "What's that? And that? And that over there?" Huzzy had all the answers. She identified each plant with each name sounding more interesting than the one before it.

"Torchwood," Huzzy called the yellow-flowered shrub. "Bracken. Turk's cap mallow. Butterfly orchid. Buttonbush."

"There are so many different kinds. So many different shapes and colors," Shawn marveled.

"Ah, yes," Huzzy said, spotting some trees that were interesting to look at but would also be useful to them. "And here is the wild almond tree and over here a carissa."

"Those look like plums," Shawn said, reaching for one of the fiery red fruits. "Ouch!" She pulled back her hand. A sharp thorn had stuck her finger as she tried to pick a plum. Before she could make too much of the small drop of blood, her attention was pulled to a tiny hummingbird hovering in place in front of one of the starlike blossoms on the tree. "Fruit, thorns, flowers, and hummingbirds all in one place!" she said excitedly. "Oh, Huzzy, this is a paradise, isn't it?"

Huzzy knew what Shawn was feeling. It was

the charm of the islands coming over her the same way it came over those who lived on them. There was no escaping that once one had been caught by it. That was a fact Huzzy knew from all the stories told of people who had come to the islands looking for some new meaning in life. Some kept going. But some stayed and never left. It was said that they had been captured by some mysterious charm.

"We must keep going a little." Huzzy smiled. "But we will come back again."

Shawn wanted to stop and make some sketches of the different leaves and flowers, but she knew Huzzy was right. She walked on behind Huzzy and was surprised at how easily the girl on the awkward crutch swung her swollen foot forward. Suddenly Huzzy stopped.

"What is it?" Shawn asked.

Huzzy pointed to a strange-looking pothole to the left of the fern-covered path. In the pothole there appeared to be water. Shawn rushed ahead to the spot and started to dip a finger into the water. With just a drop on her fingertip she tasted it. "It's fresh!" she cried out. "Huzzy! It's fresh water!" Before Huzzy could answer, Shawn cupped her two hands together and dipped deeper into the hole. She drank thirstily from her hands and immediately spit out all she had taken in.

"Salty?" Huzzy laughed. "Yes. I was afraid

that might be so. We have these small wells here that have fresh water on the surface, but below there is a bed of salt. Too bad. We will keep looking, though."

The two girls walked ahead another fifteen or twenty feet and came to another larger pool of water. "Want to taste it, Shawn?" Huzzy said, laughing her hearty laugh.

Shawn laughed, too. "I think I'll take it a little more slowly this time," she said, dipping a finger in.

"Wait a minute, please," Huzzy said, checking around the vegetation that grew alongside the pool. She looked for signs of poisonous plants and saw none to worry about. "Go ahead. And this time I will test it with you." She stuck her crutch out to one side and balanced on one foot as she bent down. First a drop on a finger and then a handful of the clear, cool water proved it to be exactly what they were looking for.

Shawn looked over at Huzzy. Huzzy looked at Shawn. Both smiled broadly as they agreed. "Fresh!" they said at the same time.

"We are in luck!" Huzzy said, feeling better for the first time that day. With water on the island, fish in the sea, and fruits on the trees, Huzzy knew one thing: If they had to, they could survive on Chilas Cay.

6.
Home Fires

Libby was the first to hear the two explorers' footsteps crackling through the leafy pathway back to the clearing. She jumped up quickly and ran to meet them. "What did you see?" she asked anxiously. "Are there any other people?"

"Are there wild animals in the woods?" asked Annie, not really wanting to hear the answer if it was "yes."

"We did not see wild animals, Annie," Huzzy said, getting rid of those fears right away. "And no, I do not believe there are any people sharing their island with us." She saw a look of disappointment come over their faces. Before tears could gather, she said, "But we do have some good news. We have found fresh water!"

"Oh, Huzzy," Sarah said seriously. "That's wonderful. Really wonderful."

"Yes," agreed Huzzy, "and so is what you have done here." She and Shawn had left the others with a total mess. In the short time they'd been gone, Sarah had magically turned the piles of things into the makings of a homey campsite.

"I thought it best if we all kept busy while we waited," Sarah explained, looking around and feeling satisfied with what her let's-play-*Swiss Family Robinson* game had accomplished.

Cushions from the boat were set up on boxes of supplies, making a perfect seating arrangement. In the space in the middle of the seats two large bench cushions were laid across suitcases. This "table" was already set just the way it had been for their dinner aboard the *Sea Breeze*. The red-and-white dishes and utensils on the *Windswept* placemats made it look as though they were expecting company. But the empty horizon on the ocean backdrop told Huzzy that no company would be coming *this* night.

When Sarah had seen Annie and Libby growing tearful again as they waited for Huzzy and Shawn to return, she put her own worries aside and invented the game. "I know!" she said, forcing cheerfulness on them. "We'll pretend we really are the Robinson family, and we'll try to make our place as beautiful as they made theirs."

Both girls welcomed the distraction even if they didn't wholly believe the game.

"Even if we're only going to be here for one night," she said, "I'll still need a kitchen to cook dinner in." And then the three of them worked together to arrange supplies in a U-shape to create the kitchen space. At the top of the U, Sarah dug a hole and laid dried brush and branches in it to make a fireplace for cooking. Libby set the table while Annie gathered palmetto branches and wove them into a kind of carpet for the kitchen floor.

"Isn't that the most beautiful floor you've ever seen?" Sarah said to Huzzy when she saw her looking at it. "Annie made it!"

Annie rolled her eyes in exasperation. All she'd done was lay one branch going this way, the next one going that way, the next one going this way until she'd made a floor of palm leaves. It wasn't such a big deal.

"Oh, Anniekins," Sarah went on, still playing the Swiss Family mother, "you're so clever I could just eat you up!"

"Yes," said Shawn, "it does look nice." She smiled at Annie as she remembered what the younger girl had said on the dock that first day when they both watched the pelican swallow a fish whole.

"The pelican reminds me of my sister, and I'm the fish," she'd said. "Sarah's always threatening to eat me up whenever I do something too incredible for words."

Shawn had put an arm around Annie at the time because she understood exactly what Annie meant. She herself had felt the sting of false praise about her artwork in a home filled with even greater artists. She knew that sometimes words of encouragement could be overdone.

But Huzzy really did think the girls had done a remarkable job. She saw the bottles of water neatly stacked, the chilly bins with the meat and perishable foods packed tightly inside, the cooking utensils and kitchenware arranged perfectly on mats made of ferns, and all the other food goods in order for easy access. It was clear to Huzzy that Sarah had turned the situation into a game, and she hoped the girls would all be willing to play a while longer. As she surveyed the setup, she did not see Allison right away.

"Where is our Allison?" she asked with concern.

"She's down on the beach watching for a boat to come. She's been there ever since you left," Annie answered.

Huzzy stood for a moment watching Allison watching the water. The girl sat still as a bird caught in the sight of a cat. "If there is a boat," Huzzy said softly, "she will surely see it."

A hissing sizzling sound brought her attention back to the kitchen. Sarah had started a fire in the fireplace and was starting to fry chicken for their dinner.

"That smells good," Shawn said, looking over Sarah's shoulder. "How did you get a fire going so fast?"

"Luckily the matches were kept dry in this

Windswept plastic canister," Sarah said. "We have plenty of matches and candles so we shouldn't have to worry about keeping a fire going until we go to sleep."

"*Très bon*," Shawn said. "Very good." She turned, picked up her own things, and walked along the tree line until she was about fifty feet from where the others had parked their things. She passed Sarah's, Annie's, and Libby's belongings, which had also been arranged in a homey way. Obviously the game had been played here, too. Three mattresses were arranged in a clearing next to the kitchen area. At first Shawn thought it was Annie's boat mattress next to Sarah's. Then she saw the small picture of Libby's aunt Alice set up on a palm leaf by the bed. Next to that picture was the sketch that Shawn had drawn of Libby looking at the sunset. Shawn patted her bag of sketching things and made a mental note to herself to come back and sketch the kitchen space as well as this sleeping area. She wanted to keep a sketched record of how everything looked while they were here.

Annie's mattress was separated a little from her sister's and the others' spots. Shawn would have smiled if she'd known what Annie had been thinking when she purposely did not line her bed up with the others. "Sometimes things look a little more interesting if they don't match exactly," Shawn had said on the boat. Annie remembered that, and when Sarah laid all three mattresses out in a perfect straight line, Annie moved hers out at an angle on its own.

Allison's spot wasn't set up at all. Clearly she was not playing the game. Her mattress was up on its side, leaning against her suitcase. Only the makeup case looked as though it had been opened. This spot had the look of someone ready to leave for somewhere. Shawn laughed to herself when she looked toward the beach and saw Allison sitting on a red *Windswept* towel looking out at the ocean for a boat that wasn't coming. Poor Allison, she thought. She probably has her makeup on in case a cute guy happens to sail by.

Shawn was right. Allison sat with her eyes trained on the distant horizon. Her makeup was perfectly applied, and anyone just arriving would never have suspected that she'd just been through a terror-filled night that resulted in a shipwreck and six girls being dumped on an empty island. As soon as Sarah had started making a silly game of their tragedy, Allison walked away from it. She'd been sitting on the beach for so long now she was afraid to stop watching. She'd convinced herself that the second she took her eyes away the rescue boat would pass by and she would miss it. Though her eyes didn't wander, her mind did. She thought of home and wondered if her mother had heard yet that the great "experience-broadening" cruise had turned into a disaster. It occurred to her that anyone trying to call and let her mother know would probably give up after getting a busy signal for hours and hours.

She thought of the envelope her father had given her mother to give to her. How much money was in it she didn't know since she hadn't bothered to open it. A lot of good it will do me here! she thought.

She thought of her friends, girls and boys, and was surprised to realize she couldn't think of one who would really be missing her. Why was that? she wondered. But the fact was there wasn't one she really missed, either. Then she thought of the girls she was stuck with now. She knew they didn't like her. Who cares? she thought. Who really cares?

The blank horizon got her attention again as color began to flood it. The sun was getting lower in the sky and it blazed a fiery orange. Her green eyes teared up. Despite all her thoughts, she blamed the tears on the brightness of the setting sun. Allison gave up the watch, stood up, and started walking toward the smell of food cooking. She could see Sarah's figure bending over what looked like a fire. Just like home, she said to herself sarcastically. Only Sarah's not on the phone!

When Shawn saw Allison coming up the beach she continued walking until she found the spot where she would set up her things. She needed space, not the closeness the others seemed to need. Even though Allison had separated herself somewhat from the others, Shawn knew she'd be spreading out and spilling over into their space as soon as she realized that unpacking was the thing to do. Shawn also knew she'd found the right place the minute she saw the delicate, feathery vines of bay geraniums outlining a clearing just off the beach. As she dropped her bag down on the sand and walked into the clearing a little, her eyes saw the same kind of plum tree she'd seen with Huzzy. And this one was alive with hummingbirds attracted by the fragrant flowers. It was like a fairyland tree with the colorful, tiny birds decorating it. This tree would be the center of her space, she decided, and her shelter would be built around it. She was not going to play games. She was not going to watch the water for nothing. As long as they were on this island, Shawn was going to make herself at home, and secretly she hoped no boat would come for a long, long time.

Taking out her sketch pad, Shawn began to draw her ideas for how her shelter would look. Once she did that she made a list of things she would need to make it the way she wanted it: sailcloth, shells, palm leaves, and flowers. Just as she finished her list, her name came drifting down the beach on the evening breeze. She looked up and saw Sarah waving to her to come to dinner. Again taking her sketching things along, Shawn walked back to where the others were busily getting the food onto the table.

"What's way down there?" Annie asked Shawn, pointing to where Shawn had left her things.

"That's where I have chosen to make my shelter," Shawn replied. "It's a beautiful spot. I think I'll be quite comfortable there."

"Comfortable?" Allison growled. "Now there's a word I haven't thought of since we left home."

The mention of the word *home* took Libby out of "the game," and the pain of missing everything she knew stabbed her. She thought of her aunt Alice home alone, surely by now knowing that something terrible had happened to her niece. Libby could just picture the kind woman walking sadly around the house, feeling afraid to leave in case the phone call came. She'd had a phone call like what this one would be when Libby's parents had died. Suddenly Libby felt another feeling: guilt. How could she put her aunt through another tragedy? If only she could just let the woman know that she was all right. Well, so far, anyway.

"The chicken is ready," Sarah said, ignoring Allison's reminder of home.

Real hunger seemed to grab all the girls at once, and they pushed each other to find places at the makeshift table. Sarah served each of them one piece of chicken, and they immediately attacked it, holding it in their hands and tearing the meat off with their teeth. "Wait a minute, please!" Sarah said, holding up one hand. Her motherly voice took over. "I know we're all hungry, but our thanks should come first." She bowed her head and the others reluctantly put down their food and followed her example. Sarah spoke softly. "Thank you for delivering us safely to this island. Keep us safe from harm and please, let us get home safely as well. Amen."

Without speaking the girls went back to the attack, savoring each bite of meat as though it were their last. They did not stop to wipe their mouths or hands. They did not stop for anything until the last of it was gone. Huzzy ate more slowly than the others, saving hers in case one of her girls needed more. Sarah had a surprise for them, though. When the chicken was gone she handed out chocolate bars that she'd gathered from the *Windswept* tote bags.

"Dessert!" she said, cheerfully. And somehow as she watched all of them sitting with the sunset behind them eating such a civilized thing as candy bars, the game changed for her. Now she felt like Wendy in *Peter Pan*. Here were her children and she was their mother. It wasn't

real, of course. Just a game, she thought com-
fortingly to herself. Just a game, that's all.

Shawn was the first to stand up. "Before the
sun goes down I have to get my bed set up and
get some other things down to where I'm staying," she said.

"I'll help you take your stuff," Annie volunteered, jumping up from the table. She was tired
of Sarah's game and wanted to get away from
it.

"Yes," Huzzy said, "I, too, must prepare my
sleeping place."

"I'll help you," Libby said. "It might be hard
for you with that foot."

"Indeed," agreed Huzzy. "This foot of mine is
some bad luck, but a sprain is not the worst
thing. I think I can do something for it."

The girls were a little mystified, but by this
time they knew Huzzy was full of interesting
information and unusual customs. "What do you
mean, Huzzy?" Sarah asked.

"Libby, perhaps you can help me with my ankle by finding me a bit of rope. Not the nylon
lines. I will need one of the hemp ropes from the
boat, the brown ones." Huzzy pointed to where
Sarah had neatly coiled ropes and lines, and
folded the sails and sail bags. While Libby went
for rope, Huzzy turned to Shawn. "Have you
any turpentine with your art supplies?" she
asked.

"Sure," Shawn said reaching into her bag and pulling out a small bottle. She handed it to Huzzy and watched curiously to see what she would do with it.

All the girls gathered around their leader and silently observed as Huzzy picked out strands of hemp from the twisted rope Libby had found. She laid the strands out straight on a big sea grape leaf and poured turpentine on them. Then she began to wrap her ankle in the soaked strands, dabbing on a little more turpentine once the ankle was bound up. "You see, my girls," she said as she worked, "the oakum with the turpentine will work to heal the sprain more quickly."

"Oakum?"

"That is the name for the strands of hemp," Huzzy explained. "There are many medicines that do not come by way of a doctor," she continued. "Right here on the island we can find many cures for many sicknesses, but one must know the plants well."

"Well," Libby said softly, "is there a plant to cure homesickness?"

Huzzy answered seriously as her father would have at a moment like this. She took Libby's chin in her hand, looked her in the eye, and said, "Libby, some cures must come from within. It must be your own strength that heals that kind of sickness."

All the girls listened when Huzzy spoke in that tone. She spoke with a kind of wisdom, a kind of certainty that made them feel safe and protected even though their situation was so frightening in reality. Huzzy saw this look of trust in their eyes and promised herself that she would be worthy of that trust. The muscles in her jaw tightened as the burden of responsibility closed in on her. She knew the eyes on her were looking for some reassurance that they would be safe and they would be saved. She looked down at her newly bound ankle, then up at the girls again and said brightly, "Now you see, my girls, even away from home we have home remedies."

"And home cooking!" Sarah added. Then she played *Peter Pan*'s Wendy again. "All right, everyone," she said clapping her hands together. "We'd better finish cleaning up here so our camp is all neat and tidy before bedtime."

Allison and Annie groaned at the same time. Both were thinking they could survive a night on this island, but could they survive a night with Sarah acting like everyone's mother? Well, thought Allison, by tomorrow there's sure to be someone coming for us. Nobody really gets lost in this day and age. She looked over just in time to see Sarah starting to cover the fire with sand. "No! Don't!" she yelled out. "Don't put the fire out!"

"It's all right, Allison," Sarah said. "We have plenty of matches."

"No!" Allison yelled again. "How will anyone see us at night if we don't keep a fire going?"

"She's right," Libby said. "Please, Sarah. Don't put it out."

Seeing the fear in their faces, Huzzy soothed Allison and Libby with a different idea. "You know," she began, "my Mama Selina often told of the times when she was a young girl on the islands. One of my favorite stories was of the fishermen who would leave before the sun came up, carrying their fishing nets over their shoulders. They would go off on fishing boats made of mahogany and dogwood trees. Sometimes these boats would be as long as thirty-five feet. Big enough to carry all the men in the village. During the day the men would be gone and the women would wait for their return. Too often darkness came before they did. Mama told of the beauty of the home fires that burned brightly all along the beach so the men would not pass by their homes, but would safely find their way back. Perhaps we need these same fires along our beach, yes?"

She didn't have to work to convince anyone of it. They quickly finished the clean-up duties. Annie and Shawn agreed to come back and help with the fires as soon as Shawn's place was set up. Libby helped Huzzy set her place up near enough to the other girls so she could watch over them, but separate enough to allow herself the space and privacy needed to think. Allison just threw her mattress down outside the circle of three and didn't even attempt to make it look any more than temporary.

By the time the orange sun had turned the sky to pink, then deep lavender, and finally navy-blue dotted with millions of white stars, six home fires burned along the beach. The embers of the fires shed a warm glow and a warm feeling over the girls who lay on their mattresses staring into the fires instead of into the night. Huzzy sang her island songs for them, starting with a funny one about a boy who listened for the sound of the ocean in a shell. He cried because he couldn't hear it over the sound of the real ocean. She sang fast songs about fishermen and sailors and fish that got away. Her singing helped them to forget for the moment that they were in fact lost.

In the glow of her own fire, Shawn sat bent over her sketch pad drawing the scene she saw from her separate place. Her picture showed five fires: first one, then three clustered together, then another one. Her fire was not included. She drew a background of tall island pines silhouetted against a night sky, and in the foreground were the faces of five girls seemingly floating above the ghostly glow of their individual fires. She could see their faces clearly.

Allison kept her face turned to the sea, obviously still looking for rescuers. Libby looked into the fire as though it were a crystal ball with some answers about their future in it. Annie sat looking over at her sister whose hair had a perfect halo-glow of its own in the firelight. Sarah sat smiling her perfect smile at Libby and Annie. And as Huzzy sang her songs she seemed to be looking down the beach to where Shawn sat.

The last of Huzzy's songs was the same one she had sung for Libby to help her sleep. With Shawn watching, this time the soft song lulled all of them to sleep, even Huzzy herself. Now Shawn felt really alone. She thought of Huzzy's story of the home fires burning for the men coming in from the sea. She looked out at the dark ocean and saw no one. Good, she thought. I'm not ready to be found yet.

Then, just in case someone was out there looking for signs of the lost girls, Shawn quickly threw sand over her fire. "There," she whispered to herself when the last ember was buried. "That's better."

Now she felt safe.

7.
Out of Reach

Sunlight and birds' songs worked together to wake up the girls. But the light was a lot brighter than some of their moods. Even in a still clearing, Allison felt like she had been rocking all night long. Libby had dreams of drowning. Annie felt itchy just worrying about lizards crawling on her. And Sarah felt responsible. She decided being cheery was easier when one didn't have to be, and games became work when the choice of whether or not to play was taken away. Morning did not bring a parade of happy rescuers to the island. It brought hunger. Somehow working in "the kitchen" didn't seem such a fun idea to Sarah this second day.

Annie was quickest to stand up because she was anxious to shake off the imaginary things that had walked on her all night. "Yeecch!" she said, brushing nothing away but feeling better for it. "Hey, where's Huzzy?"

"Down there on the other side of those rocks,"

Allison said, not even looking up from the mirror she held in one hand while she put on eyeliner with the other. "She's with Shawn and it looks like they've found something. I hope it's a plane ticket out of here." She dabbed on some eyeshadow and was finished. "A one-way plane ticket straight out of here," she said again.

Remembering the dreams she'd had in the night, Libby answered Allison seriously. "I'm sure it's not that," she said. "We won't be leaving here today. I know that." She looked over at the picture Shawn had drawn of her on the *Sea Breeze* and remembered how homesick she'd felt that night after telling the story of her parents' accident. Until now, Libby hadn't noticed the way Shawn had made the orange of her hair blend into the orange sky background, as though she were melting into the sunset. Her dream had been like that, too, she suddenly realized, but in her dream her whole body seemed to melt and blend in with the ocean. In her mind she kept seeing herself becoming a part of this island in the same way, just gradually melting into it. Libby knew she was doing that again; letting her thoughts get carried away by fear and worry.

"Libby? Libby, are you all right?" Sarah's hand on her hair pulled Libby out of her thoughts. "You look lost in thought."

"Lost?" Libby said, snapping out of it. "Oh, yes, I guess I am."

"I guess we all are," Annie said.

"Well, one thing that isn't lost is our appetites," Sarah said, bringing the subject around to one she felt more comfortable with. She was ready to play "the game" again. "How about some breakfast?" she said in her best Wendy voice.

Just then Huzzy's voice called out to them. The girls looked down near the water and saw Huzzy waving with the arm that wasn't leaning on the oar crutch.

"I think she wants us," said Sarah.

Huzzy held something up in the air, but they were too far away to see what it was. Then Shawn held up the same thing, whatever it was. Both of them seemed excited, and Huzzy called to them again.

As Sarah, Libby, and Annie ran out of the clearing and down the sandy beach, Allison's curiosity got the better of her. She followed at her own pace. Slowly. When she finally caught up with the others they had already reached the point by the cratered volcanic rocks where the *Sea Breeze* could still be seen just below the surface. Now they were following the sound of Huzzy's voice, which came from the other side of the rocks.

"Over on this side, girls!" she sang out cheerfully. "We have made a discovery!"

Clinging to each other, the four girls climbed

carefully over the pinkish-brown rocks. As they stood on top of the rocks and looked down they saw an incredible sight.

"What are they?" Allison asked.

"There must be hundreds of them!" Annie said.

Huzzy stood leaning on her crutch smiling a broad smile. "Conch!" she said proudly holding up a big gray shell in one hand. In the shallow water at her feet the ocean bed was covered with more of the big shells.

Noticing the way the water flowed between two rocky walls, Annie called out, "It's a Conch Canyon!"

"That is a perfect name for this place, Annie," Huzzy said. "And why not come down here into the canyon to find a big conch of your own? We will have a wonderful breakfast this morning, yes?"

Sarah looked worried. "I don't know how to cook conch," she said.

"That may be the best news of the day," Allison said disgustedly. The great gray shells that looked like breakfast to Huzzy only looked like trouble to Allison. The thought of eating whatever was in one of those shells practically made her gag.

Shawn wasn't in the water. But she wasn't missing the moment, either. She had planted herself on a flat part of the rocks and was sketching the sea of conch and Huzzy holding up her prize catch. Looking down from the rocks above, the other four girls stood admiring Huzzy's find. Once again, Shawn had left herself out of the scene, but with the hundreds of shells she felt the picture was full enough.

"I have a shell like that at home," Annie said. "But it's much prettier than these. It's pink and white and very shiny. You can hear the ocean in it."

Huzzy explained that the gray shells did polish up to a shiny pink or coral color when they were cleaned of the conch living inside. "The shell is the home of the conch, but it is also alive. When the conch dies, so does the shell. Then it hardens and may be polished."

"But how do you get the conch to come out of the shell?" Libby asked.

"Hoh," laughed Huzzy. "He will not come out. We must take him out. Here, you take this one from me while I climb back up. This foot is no better today I am afraid." She struggled a little to get her crutch up and then herself.

"What about the oakum and turpentine?" Annie asked. "Didn't that work?"

"Well, Annie," Huzzy replied, "I said the foot is no better, but it is not worse, either, so I think I must say it did work. The swelling might have been much greater if I had not kept it down with my Mama Selina's remedy. Come now, shall we?

I will show you all how we get this conch out of the shell and into our stomachs."

Even Allison and Sarah, who didn't like the idea of eating one, were curious about how a conch was removed. They all followed Huzzy back up the beach to their camp. Shawn followed, carrying her sketch pad and an empty conch shell she'd found. Immediately Huzzy spread out a big palm leaf and got out a knife and chipping hammer from the boat's toolbox. The girls watched her crack a tiny hole at the pointed end of the shell. Then with the narrow knife she reached inside the hole and released the conch's grip on the inside of the shell. She quickly turned the shell over in her hand and easily pulled the conch out of the front of the shell. Using the knife again, Huzzy cut off what she called the "slops," skinned and scraped the conch, and cut it up into small pieces. She popped one cleaned piece into her mouth, causing all of the girls to gasp.

"Would you like to try a piece?" Huzzy asked, holding up another bite to anyone who dared to try it.

"Doesn't it need to be cooked?" Sarah asked.

"It is good many ways," Huzzy answered. "Raw, boiled, steamed, in a cut-up, a soup, a stew. Quite delicious, really."

Shawn reached out and took the raw piece from Huzzy's outstretched hand. She popped it into her mouth the same way Huzzy did. All the girls watched, expecting Shawn to spit it out. She didn't. A smile spread over her face as she chewed and the sweet, fishy taste filled her mouth. "It's good," she said. "Really good."

None of the others would try it raw or cooked, so Sarah took eggs out of one of the coolers and opened another to take out the bacon. When the meat cooler was opened a bad smell hit Sarah in the nose. It was a rotten smell, and although she didn't want to do it, she put her nose closer to the meats inside.

"Oh, no," Sarah said. "This can't be." She started pulling out packages of ground beef, chicken, chops, and steak, smelling each of them and looking sicker by the minute. "How did this happen?"

"What is it, Sarah?" Huzzy asked. But now the rotten smell had reached her nose as well, and in fact all the girls covered their noses and mouths so they wouldn't breathe in the awful odor.

"It's all gone bad," Sarah said. "All the meat is bad." She twisted her hands together in a nervous motion and repeated her discovery. "It's all rotten!"

"Here is the trouble," Huzzy said, pointing at a hole in the back of the cooler. "It must have broken in the storm. Bad luck. We will have to bury this somewhere away from our camp."

"What will we eat?" Allison cried, her throat beginning to feel as if it was closing up. "We'll all starve if they don't come for us today!"

"No," Huzzy corrected in a sure, calm voice. "We will not starve. We will eat fruit. We will eat fish. We will eat this." She held up another piece of raw conch. "Sarah, you must boil water so we can cook our breakfast now."

Sarah did as she was told and, when the water came to a boil, she dropped the cut-up pieces of conch into the water. She was surprised to see it firm up and turn white just like scallops or other seafood with which she was more familiar. After several minutes, she scooped out a piece with a spoon, blew on it, and offered it to Annie or Libby first.

"No, thanks, you have it," Libby said solemnly.

"And if you live, we'll try it," Annie added, wrinkling her nose as her sister took a tiny bite.

Sarah held the piece in her mouth for a minute and then swallowed it whole. Already she missed the meat, but she tried another small bite. This time she chewed it and was surprised at the mild taste. In fact, it didn't have too much taste at all, and that was a great relief to her. The last thing she wanted to do was make the younger girls worry about the food they were going to have to eat sooner or later.

While Annie and Libby set the table for breakfast, Sarah served eggs and conch to those who wanted it. Only Allison refused to even try the shellfish. She just picked at the eggs and seemed distracted by her need to keep watching the ocean for a rescue boat.

Shawn ate quickly, took her plate down to the water to wash it, and then took her shell and sketch pad back to her place down the beach. She stayed there for hours, only leaving to gather more flowers, shells, and palm leaves to complete the shelter she'd begun the day before. She didn't notice or care what the others were up to. She was happy to be left alone while Allison went back to her spot down by the water and the others went with Huzzy to find fruits.

Sarah was back in her game. She had no choice. It was the only way she could keep from thinking about what they might lose next. She didn't want to let her mind dwell on thoughts of home, her parents and how they must be feeling right now, and what would happen next. The boat was gone. Now the meat was gone. What would happen when all the supplies were gone? What would happen if the boat Allison watched for never came? Sarah stopped herself. "We'll bring our *Windswept* tote bags to gather fruits in," she said changing the subject for herself. "Each of us can carry a bag and we can get enough to last for . . ."

"For what?" Libby asked.

"For however long we need it," Sarah answered.

"We will carry what we need for today," Huzzy said, coming up behind them. "And we will know where to get more if we need it." Once again, Huzzy led the way through the clearing, but this time she showed the girls how to trample down the low brush and lay palmetto leaves over it to make the path totally clear all the way to the fresh water. They passed the salty pothole of water, but Shawn had already told them of her mistake, so they kept walking. While Annie and Libby trampled brush, Sarah and Huzzy laid down the leaves. Soon the path to the fresh water was done.

"A pool!" sang out Libby at the sight of the small pond.

"More like a sink," Annie corrected her. The others laughed, but as they gathered around the small freshwater pool, the laughter turned to silence and sighs as each of them realized that the pool was only a reminder of yet another convenience of home they would be without.

Annie looked at her sister, waiting for Sarah to say something cheerful in her game-playing voice, something that would make them believe that if they just thought lovely thoughts they could fly out of here. Sarah said nothing. Annie looked to Huzzy, but Huzzy had shifted her attention to trying to reach a high plum with the end of her oar-crutch.

"I think I can get it," Libby said, putting a hand on a thorny branch and pulling it back suddenly.

"Yes," Huzzy said, "watch for thorns. That is why I was using my crutch."

"Here, maybe this will help," Annie said, picking up a leafy palm branch. "Maybe I can just kind of wave it down."

Soon all the girls were going after the one big plum that was so out of reach. All of them had found palm branches and were waving them back and forth, creating a breeze for each other as well as for the plum that wouldn't come down. As the palm fans brushed against faces and caused both Annie and Libby to fall backward on top of each other, the girls found themselves laughing. For the moment they forgot they were lost. The giggles and squeals when smaller plums fell and left round purple juice stains on their arms and clothes, filled the grove. Soon the plum hunt turned to a fan fight, with the girls waving the giant fans at each other until laughter made them all surrender.

"Shhh!" Huzzy suddenly said. "Hush, girls!" She stopped her fan's rustle and stood with her head cocked and one ear turned to the sky.

Now the others caught the sound, too. A low

buzzing came from somewhere above the trees and off toward the other side of the island. It was a humming that at first sounded like it could have been coming from a hive of bees or a whole flock of hummingbirds. They all stood as still as they could, but the sound seemed lost now. "What was it?" Sarah whispered.

"Shhh!" Huzzy said again, straining her ears to hear and her eyes to see through the web of tree leaves overhead. Bits of sky showed through the crisscross of branches, and streaks of sunlight shot down to the ground like laser beams. But she could see nothing that would explain the sound that was gone now.

Libby held onto Sarah's arm and nervously bit her lip as she watched Huzzy watching the sky. It could have been bees, she thought. Or birds. Still none of them moved. Sarah put an arm around Libby. Annie kept her eyes on Sarah, hoping to see a look of understanding on her sister's face.

"There it is again!" Sarah breathed.

The same low buzz came again from somewhere in the far distance, but this time there was no mistaking it for what it was.

Now Allison's voice could be heard shouting from down the path the girls had cleared. As she got closer and closer to where they were, her words became clear. "A plane!" she cried. "Did you hear it? A plane!" She was breathless from running but did not want to stop. Using her bare hands to thrash the brush in front of her, Allison pushed past the girls, shouting, "Help me clear the way! It's on the other side!"

Now they were all beating the brush and bashing it back with their hands, with their feet, as Huzzy used her crutch. The growth on the other side of the pool was thicker and more jungle-like, but Allison's desperate attacks on the dense, natural barricade made all of them work harder to break through it. Thorns pricked them, thin, sharp sticks stabbed them, and dried vines hanging down scratched their faces and arms until all of them bled.

"Keep going!" Allison commanded, salty tears stinging the cuts on her face.

Now the buzzing was louder and closer, but still it was somewhere on the other side of the jungle. "It is a plane!" shouted Libby. "They're looking for us!" She couldn't see it, but the buzzing had become a real engine sound. She just knew if they could only get the rest of the way through the wall of vines they'd be able to see the plane. And the plane would be able to see them.

Allison was at the head of the group with her hair tangling in the low branches and her clothes tearing on the rough bark. She didn't care about her hair or her clothes or her body that was being torn as easily as her blouse. All she cared about was getting through to the other side before it was too late. The buzzing seemed to be circling now at one end of the island. Then it faded as the plane flew out over the water and turned again back to the beach. Allison's hands were full of thorny splinters, tears flooded her eyes, making the way even harder to see, but finally she was through it, and the pathway was clear again as it had been on the other side of the pool.

"Wait!" screamed Allison as she ran the obstacle course of palmetto trees. The buzzing was loudest now as the plane flew the length of the beach toward which Allison was running. "We're here! You've found us!" she shouted, the tears streaming pink down her face as they washed the cuts on the way down her cheeks. "We're here!" she screamed as at last she reached the tree line at the edge of the sand. But the plane was heading away and to the other end of the island. Allison stood on the beach in clear sight waving her arms and screaming again, "We're here! Don't go! We're right here!"

Now the others had caught up with her in time to see the plane going to the other side and then out to sea again. All of them waved their arms and shouted, but it was no use.

Allison collapsed in a heap and could not stop the tears. Sarah and Annie and Libby held onto each other the way they had in the storm, and waited for calm to come back to them. Huzzy stood still, watching the sky where the plane had been. Then she turned and saw her girls. These girls who only a few days earlier had stood before her looking bright and eager for the adventure that lay ahead, now stood looking tattered and torn by the adventure they were in.

Solemnly, Huzzy collected her group like so many shells. Their energy was gone, used up in the battle with the brush, but somehow she was able to get them on the now-cleared path. They followed without speaking, stopping only to pick up the bags they'd dropped in the race. Plums lay on the ground where they'd had the fan fight, and now Sarah suddenly began to collect the bruised fruits as though they were treasures.

"We might need them," she said in a breathy voice. "Take them all, Annie. We'll need them all." She scurried around like a squirrel gathering nuts for the winter, and she didn't know when to stop or when enough was enough.

"That is it," Huzzy said quietly. "We can come back another time. The fruits will still be here."

"And so will we," whispered Allison. "So will we."

When the plane flew over, Shawn could not move. Her arms were loaded down with palmetto branches, shells, pink and white flower blossoms, and flat stones, all things she'd gathered to use in the making of her shelter. She heard the buzzing coming from somewhere off in the distance. At first she thought it was the sound of the hummingbirds that fluttered magically in place around the flowering plum tree in her clearing. By the time she believed it was a plane and not the birds, it was too late. The sound had drifted to the other side of the island and then out of her hearing. "If they came once, they'll come again," she said aloud to a tiny lizard who looked as much a part of the tree as the bark on which he sat.

She was almost finished with the work she'd been doing for hours, and the things she held in her arms were just the final touches. Carefully she placed each item where she wanted it, then stood back to look at what she had done. She was pleased.

What she saw before her was a fairy-tale scene that stood out like a castle in the clouds of some fairy-tale sky. At the base of a flowering plum tree, a tent made of bright white sailcloth hung like an awning from the low branches of the tree. The tent was open on three sides, and tiny hummingbirds fluttered magically in place, drinking sweet nectar from the blossoms. They flitted from bloom to bloom, sometimes taking a shortcut through the tent. Painted on the open tent flaps were bouquets of pink and lavender flower blossoms that matched the real flowers scattered over the palmetto-leafed walkway and tent floor.

She had been right. The sound of buzzing was coming again. Shawn looked up and didn't see a plane, but a movement further down the beach caught her eye. It was Allison running from her lookout spot in the direction of the buzzing sound. She seemed to be shouting as she pointed at the sky and ran into the clearing behind the camp area. Shawn listened for a while until the buzzing sound disappeared completely.

Annie's voice coming up behind her startled Shawn. "There was a plane," Annie said breathlessly. She stood panting from running. "Did you see it? Did you hear it?"

"I did hear it," Shawn said calmly. She turned around and gasped when she saw Annie's scratched and bleeding face and arms. Her clothes were torn, and her hair was full of bits of leaves and brush. "Oh, Annie, what happened to you?" Shawn asked worriedly.

"We ran," Annie explained, still out of breath from running to find out where Shawn was. "But we were too late."

"I was too late, too," Shawn said. "But don't worry, Annie. There'll be another one."

Annie wished she could be sure that Shawn was right. Certainly Shawn looked calm enough, so she must believe what she was saying. Then for the first time Annie noticed Shawn's tent. "Oh! Look what you did!" she exclaimed. "You made a house!" Suddenly Annie felt all mixed up. While she and the others were running to get the attention of the plane to take them off the island, Shawn was making a place that didn't look temporary at all! "But why are you making a house here?" Annie asked. "It's so beautiful just to tear down when we leave." Annie didn't understand.

"And I've just finished the beginning of my counting wall," Shawn said, pointing to the two shells.

"Counting wall?" Annie almost whispered.

"Yes," explained Shawn matter-of-factly. "Each day we're here I'll add another shell. Just so I can keep track of our days on the island."

"A counting wall!" Now it was Sarah's voice coming up behind them both. She had come for Annie. When Huzzy led them through the clearing after seeing the plane, Allison just kept walking right back to her lookout spot at the water's edge. Libby fell exhausted onto her mattress, stared into the face of her aunt Alice's picture, and tried to find comfort there. Huzzy's throbbing foot needed a rest so she sat leaning against a tree. But Sarah had to keep busy. Still moving like a panicked squirrel, she emptied the bags of fruits. Then she arranged them one way and changed the arrangement again and again. When she turned to ask Annie to help, Annie was gone. So Sarah walked up the beach and found her with Shawn talking about this counting wall of shells.

"There isn't going to be any wall," Sarah said firmly. "There was a plane. Didn't you see it? Didn't you hear it? They're looking for us. They'll be coming back. There isn't going to be any wall here. Walls are permanent, and this is just a temporary situation. Come back with me now, Annie."

Shawn just looked at Sarah. Then she turned to Annie and said, "Each night before supper I will add another shell to the wall. You can help if you like."

Annie didn't know what to say. She felt pulled by both girls, but Shawn released her when she said, "I'll come back with you to the camp. I need to get more shells for the wall."

Sarah chose to ignore the mention of the wall again. Instead she changed the subject abruptly to supper and talked about making plum tarts out of the plums they'd found earlier. "Yes," she said in a distracted way. "That should keep us busy for a while. We'll make tarts."

All the rest of the daylight hours that day, and then by the light of the home fires that night, Sarah baked. The island was filled with the sweet smell of plums cooking. Daylight came again, and Sarah still boiled plums for the tarts she made. Nothing could take her from her baking. She seemed not to hear any talk of the plane that had come, of the boat that was gone, of anything. Day and night Sarah cooked. When the plums ran out, she sent Annie and Libby for more. They went without questions because they could see it was the most important thing to Sarah. She would not rest. She would not sleep. She was determined that no one would go hungry as long as she was in charge of the kitchen. So Sarah baked and baked and baked.

Finally Huzzy stopped her the same way she had stopped her from picking up plums in the grove after the plane came and went. "That is it now, Sarah," Huzzy said softly but firmly. "You have made enough tarts now."

Sarah turned from the steaming pot of boiling plums, wiped the perspiration from her tired face, and put her head down against Huzzy's chest. In Huzzy's arms, Sarah fell asleep.

8.
The Beginning

The smell of the plums stayed in the air long after Sarah had stopped cooking. Their fragrance hung heavy around the girls, weighing them down with the memory of the day plums fell around them while a plane flew away from them. They had all watched in fascinated disbelief as Sarah cooked for days and nights until she finally fell asleep standing up in Huzzy's arms. Once Huzzy laid her down, Sarah slept through the night, the next day, and the next afternoon. When she finally did wake up, her clear blue eyes had a distant look in them that Annie did not recognize.

Sarah did not wake up to play the part of Wendy, and the *Swiss Family Robinson* game seemed long forgotten. The only thing Sarah wanted to do was go to the counting wall. She wasn't sure how long she'd slept and felt the wall would give her an honest answer. Annie and Libby walked with Sarah to Shawn's shelter and arrived just in time to see Shawn in a yellow-flowered crown laying another shell down in the wall. Sarah drew in her breath as she counted eight shells and realized she had cooked and slept for so many days.

Although the counting wall belonged to Shawn, the addition of one shell each day became a ritual that belonged to all of the girls. Like the morning flag-raising ceremony at a sleepaway camp, the placing of another shell in the wall became a solemn and serious occasion every evening before supper. And every shell came to represent one more day of events in their lives away from their homes.

One shell would always be the "Plane Shell." Another marked the day Sarah stopped cooking. Another stood for a day when Libby cried all day. Still another marked the day Annie woke up to real lizards crawling on her legs, causing her to scream uncontrollably until Huzzy was finally able to comfort her with a song sung in her soothing island accent.

None of the shells meant anything to Allison except one more day of living out of a suitcase. No matter what anyone said, she refused to take her things out. When the plane came back or when the rescue boat came for them, she intended to be ready. "I'll never be comfortable here," she told the others when they asked why she didn't at least try to make her sleeping area a little more homey. "So why try to pretend that I am?"

"What's the difference if you pretend to be comfortable or if you pretend someone is coming to save us?" Annie challenged Allison.

Allison exploded and a blast of angry words hit Annie in the face. "I'm not pretending that!" she screamed. "It's true. Of course the plane will come back! Or a boat will come! No one just lets six girls get lost without trying to find them. I'm the only one who's watching, and I'll be the only one ready when they get here!"

Annie shouted back at her attacker. "All you do is sit and watch, but you didn't even see the plane when it *did* come!"

Allison raised an open hand to slap Annie, but Huzzy reached out her own hand and caught Allison by the wrist. "Allison!" Huzzy boomed. "Stop this!"

"Well, it's true, Huzzy," Allison said, breaking down in tears. "I'm the only one who isn't pretending around here. I light the fires and keep them going so we'll be seen at night. I sit and watch that stupid water and that stupid sky all day. I'm not pretending someone will find us. Someone *will* come. That has to be real! What isn't real is Sarah making tarts and playing games all the time. What *isn't* real is Princess Plum down the beach there living in a flowered cocoon, building a wall around herself! But what *is* real, what's *really* real is that we are *lost*. We are six girls who are really, really lost!"

Allison was finished.

For the first time since they'd been on the island, Sarah cried. And for the first time since they'd been on the island, Libby didn't. Instead, both Libby and Annie put an arm around Sarah and tried to comfort her. While they did that, Huzzy followed after Allison who had turned and walked back to her place at the water's edge.

From where Shawn sat at the opening of her white tent, she could see Huzzy down by the shore with an arm around Allison. Over by the kitchen, Sarah seemed surrounded by the two younger girls. Shawn sketched what she saw and added the finished drawing to the wall of drawings she had hanging inside her tent. She took a few moments to study each picture, and then sat down again and looked at her counting wall.

By the time the counting wall had reached its way around one whole side of Shawn's flowered shelter, there was still no shell marking the day of rescue. The shells gleamed in the island sun, and as the wall grew around Shawn, different kinds of walls seemed to be building up around the others. Since the night of Allison's angry outburst, talk had almost stopped. The only idle chatter on the island was the *"wichity wichy"* song of the Bahama yellowthroats as they flew around the shrubs looking for bugs.

Allison still had not unpacked. Her routine was one none of the others dared to question anymore. She got up with the sun and bathed in the warm ocean water. Then she carefully selected one of her outfits, which had all grown stiff from being washed in salt water. Last of all, Allison put on her makeup just as carefully as she would have for a day of shopping at the mall. Ready to face the day and the hope of rescue, Allison would then sit on her lookout spot and wait. Coming back only for food, she stayed there all day, every day. When evening came and it was time to light the home fires, it was always Allison who made sure the fires burned brightly and stayed lit until sunup.

Annie didn't watch the ocean. She watched Sarah. Sarah who moved in a silent trance, cooking their meals. Sarah who tucked Libby and her into bed under the stars each night. Sarah who shook the sand out of the palmetto leaf carpet. Sarah who cried. Annie had never thought her perfect sister would do that. Since the days of the plum tart cooking and now the crying, Sarah did not seem so perfect or so patient.

Libby started crying again; nothing anyone could say would stop her. All she did was cling to her watermarked picture of her aunt Alice and sob. Finally Annie snapped ferociously at her, "Knock it off!"

Sarah snapped back for Libby. "Annie! If you don't have something nice to say, don't say anything at all!"

Annie hadn't said anything at all for the last two days.

Libby hadn't meant to start crying again. It wasn't only homesickness that brought her tears back. It was a feeling of failure that made her cry. Her sweet aunt Alice had saved and saved so that Libby could have this trip. It had been so important to her that Libby have the chance to discover that she didn't have to live in fear all the time. Her aunt wanted her to be free. But freedom certainly had not come on this trip! Instead, disaster had only made her fears worse. She had been afraid to leave her aunt. She had been afraid to go on a trip alone. She had been afraid something terrible would happen to her. And hadn't she been right after all? Libby knew if she ever got home again, she would be even more of a prisoner than before. The trip had failed and so had she. She cried about it, but she didn't want to talk about it. Not to Sarah. Not to Huzzy. Not to anyone.

So it was in near-silence that the girls went through the necessary routines of getting up, getting dressed, and bathing in the ocean. In a place without rules and regulations, the girls unknowingly created their own rules and looked to Huzzy for leadership. Certain things had to be done every day. Wood and dried brush had to be gathered and stacked for the home fires. Tree food had to be gathered and stored. Conch and other fish had to be caught, cleaned, and cooked. Shelters and mattresses had to be cleaned and aired so insects would not move in, too. Garbage had to be buried. Fresh water had to be carried. None of the girls was excused from helping to get the daily chores done, and in fact, none of them resisted. Huzzy only had to ask once, and the job was done. In silence now. But done.

Of course, Huzzy noticed this new quiet that had settled over the girls. Sometimes she broke the silence by singing her songs for them. Other times she was as silent as they had become. For all the days and nights they'd been on Chilas Cay, Huzzy had chosen her words carefully. She meant to keep spirits up without getting hopes up. To keep the balance was not easy, and as the days passed and the plane did not come back, Huzzy talked less and less and thought more and more.

She had borrowed paper and pencil from Shawn and was drawing a map of the island. She knew the shape from drawings her father had made when telling the story of the wreck of

159

the *Kayaska*. Now she added things to the drawing that were not on any maps her father or grandfather had ever drawn. Huzzy's map showed the points where the home fires burned. Each girl's shelter area was shown, as well as the kitchen and table areas.

The map Huzzy drew included "Conch Canyon," the freshwater pool, the cleared path to the other side of the island, Allison's lookout, and Shawn's counting wall. The last thing Huzzy added to the map was the most difficult thing for her to add. It was the spot between the coral and the rocks where the *Sea Breeze* had gone down. As she wrote the words *Sea Breeze Sinks Here* on the spot where her boat lay drowned, she thought about the great misfortune of losing it. And she also thought about the good fortune of landing on an island, especially one on which they could survive.

Next, Huzzy thought about the sea captain who had lost his ship, too. Would there be a story told about *her* tragic loss as well, she wondered? Would there be a story told about her courage and strength and survival? She looked at her girls, silently busy with their individual chores, and respected each of them for finding their own ways of coping with a camping trip that had no end in sight. But were they coping? she worried. In the last couple of days a change had come over all of them. Although they were all together in this situation, they had become as separate from each other as the island itself was from the rest of the Abacos.

On the evening when the twenty-third shell was to be added to the counting wall, the girls came to the wall from their separate places without being called or reminded. Each knew that when the sun reached a certain point on the horizon, it was time to go to Shawn's flowery shelter to watch her silently put the next shell in place.

Allison came from her place by the water. Annie came from a high place she'd claimed above Conch Canyon. Libby and Sarah came from the kitchen area where they had been going through the food supplies and sorting out fruits that had rotted. And last of all came Huzzy, still using the crutch, but leaning on it less every day.

For Shawn, the ritual of building the wall served two purposes. It was a way to keep track of days spent away from home, but it was also her way of counting the days that she belonged to the island. There was a difference in her mind. Being away from home did not necessarily mean home became the place where one was. But for Shawn, the more days spent on the island, the more at home she felt. She did not watch for rescue boats or planes. She watched for dolphins. She watched for new flowers to grow where she had picked others. And she watched for changes in the colors of the ocean and sky, and then she sketched and painted all these things.

She laid the twenty-third shell down. Soon her entire shelter would be enclosed by the growing wall of shells. In silence the girls watched Shawn hold up a shell. Her dark tan stood out against the backdrop of the white tent as she added the next shell. As they did every evening, the girls recounted the shells in the wall and again could hardly believe that another day was turning into another night.

Without being told to do so, the girls turned one by one and walked down the beach toward the main camp to prepare the evening meal. While Libby and Annie set the table and cut up fruits, Sarah put a pot of water on the fire for the conch that Huzzy was preparing. Allison began her nightly job of lighting the home fires before dark. The only sounds were the wind through the trees and the waves rolling in and falling out to sea again.

As Huzzy held the live conch in her hands and tapped the tiny hole into the pointed end, she thought of the animal hiding inside. Against the blade of the knife she could feel it expanding inside the shell and gripping the walls of its home. The grip was tight, but with knowing hands Huzzy used the knife expertly and loosened it. She turned the shell over and easily pulled the conch out. It was easy for Huzzy because she knew how to bring the conch out.

And that is what I must do as well with my girls, Huzzy thought. I must bring them out of their shells, too, before their grips become too strong.

Looking around at the girls who had each let a wall of silence grow up around herself, Huzzy wasn't exactly sure what she should do about it. If they'd been thirsty, she would have given them a drink. If they'd been hungry, she would have given them food. But this problem was not so easy to see or to solve. They had drink. They had food. What they did not seem to have was hope, and she wondered how she could give them that? She had no idea. Then Huzzy remembered what her father said so often: "The ideas are out there for anyone to take, Huzzy. All you must do is open your mind and accept one."

Huzzy knew her father was right. There had been so many times when problems seemed too big for her to handle. But then she would think of her father's words, close her eyes, and try to imagine a sky full of ideas waiting to belong to her. It always worked. Soon one of those ideas would come to her and she would solve the problem. This is what she concentrated on all through the silent supper and afterward as she walked alone along the beach.

With only her crutch and her thoughts for company, Huzzy first walked down by the water and stared out at the sea the same way Allison did every day. It was a beautiful sight, but beauty was not enough. For a quick second Huzzy's heart leaped inside her chest as her eyes saw something moving out on the horizon. A boat? she wondered, straining her eyes to catch the sight again. The thing moved again, and then another thing, and another, and another.

"Dolphins," Huzzy said aloud. "Now they have their freedom to go, do they not?" She stood and watched them on their way to somewhere else and wished she could give them a message to carry to her home. For a minute she imagined her simple message to her father delivered on the arched back of a dolphin. It would say, "Help." And what would the message back be? Huzzy tried to guess.

She watched the waves coming in. She watched them go out again. In. Out. In again. Out again. And the next wave in had a message for her. It was the sound of her father's voice coming to her on the crest of a wave. "If you wait for things to happen, they may," said the deep voice. "If you *make* things happen, they *will*."

The voice sounded so strong and so clear in her head, it made Huzzy turn to see if perhaps her father really was there delivering the message in person. She didn't see him, but she did see all the girls from where she stood. There was no busy bustling around up near the camp.

164

They all seemed to sit like figures in an exhibit waiting to be seen, waiting for something to happen.

Suddenly Huzzy knew what she must do. The ideas were there, and she was ready to take them. She was finished with waiting for something to happen. Now, she was going to *make* something happen. With this thought driving her, Huzzy turned and hurried toward her girls. "Girls!" she called out. "Sarah! Allison! Libby! Annie! Shawn! All of you!" Huzzy could hardly keep both feet on the ground as her excitement moved her forward and she left the oar crutch behind on the beach. "Girls!"

The girls, staring hopelessly into the light of the early lit home fires, began to move from their statuelike poses as Huzzy's excited cries reached their ears. They'd never seen their leader acting so wildly out of control before, and it frightened them at first.

"What's the matter with her?" Allison was the first to say aloud.

"Is she hurt, do you think?" Sarah said, her old motherly concern surfacing again.

Before Libby or Annie could ask their own questions or make any other comments, Huzzy had reached the camp, breathless and with her black eyes blazing. Her smile gave new meaning to "ear-to-ear" as it spread beyond her face and seemed to light the entire camp.

"What is it, Huzzy?" Libby asked, feeling scared by Huzzy's loss of calm.

Huzzy didn't speak as she tore through the neatly stacked pile of ropes, sails, life jackets, and sailbags. She was like a wild woman, laughing and dancing in the fading light of day. She searched for whatever it was she seemed desperate to find.

The girls didn't know what to make of Huzzy's sudden change of mood and behavior. All they knew was she had gone for a walk on the beach and had come back on the wings of some sudden joy. Shawn heard Huzzy's laughter as it was carried to her on the back of the breeze. Curiosity brought her drifting down the beach, crowned in pink flowers and carrying her sketch pad. She didn't know what was going on, but the sight of Huzzy first dancing with a stuffed-fat sailbag, then changing partners and picking up a life jacket and giving it a whirl, was a picture Shawn had to capture. She quietly sketched as Huzzy sang and searched and the other girls watched in a stunned daze of disbelief.

At last Huzzy found what she was looking for. "The ax!" she called out, holding up a small hatchet as though it were a trophy. "Now you must follow me, girls," she ordered as she turned and ran, limping slightly, toward Conch Canyon.

"Fishing? Now?" Allison asked as they hurried to catch up with Huzzy.

Huzzy waded through the water and stood above the spot where the *Sea Breeze* had gone down. The sky was hot pink behind her, and she stood like a dark exclamation point punctuating the end of the rocky cliff. With the others standing below her, Huzzy raised the ax and brought it down on the stern of the boat, splintering the edge of the board that said *Sea Breeze*. She hammered again, causing chips to fly and land on the rocks, on the sand, and in the purple evening sea. The banging of the ax against the boat didn't stop until Huzzy was able to reach down and rip it the rest of the way. At last Huzzy held up a large, flat, wet panel that was the back of the boat.

"My girls," she said, softly now. "We are no longer going to wait for things to happen. Now we are going to *make* things happen. We are going to build a boat. It will not happen in one day. It will not happen in one week. It may not even happen in one month. But we now have the first board, and I believe, my girls, if we work together and take it one board at a time it is indeed possible."

"A boat?" Allison gasped. "Build a boat?"

"How?" Libby asked.

"With what?" Annie added.

"Yes," said Huzzy. "We are going to build a

boat, and we will use it to rescue ourselves. It will not be easy, but we have an island full of trees. We have the same sisal plants that have been turned into ropes by islanders for many years. And we have each other, yes? This is something we will do. It is something we *must* do."

As the pink sky darkened to lavender, and the island breeze softly breathed on them all, Sarah reached out an arm and pulled Annie closer to her. This time Annie didn't stiffen or pull away. With her other arm, Sarah held Libby, who leaned in but never took her eyes off Huzzy as she carefully climbed down from her rocky throne carrying the first board of their hope for escape.

Shawn heard Huzzy's words again in her mind. "It will not happen in one day. It will not happen in one week. It may not even happen in one month." She knew she still had time, and this thought was the hope she had as she joined the others on their walk back to camp.

That night, for the first time since the first night, all the girls sat together around the home fires nearest the kitchen area. This time the faces didn't float separate and alone above the fire lights. This time they sat close to each other and were a group laughing and talking happily about the boat they were going to build. As excitement turned to tiredness, Huzzy sang her softest song.

> *Little girl, little girl my own*
> *When you be sleeping*
> *You dream you be home.*
> *You dream you see your island*
> *Sitting in your hand.*
> *You dream you be home soon*
> *On your island sand.*
> *Little girl, little girl my own*
> *Soon, so soon you be*
> *On your island home.*

One by one the lost girls closed their eyes and found themselves dreaming.

But by the light of her home fire Allison thought of Huzzy's words. "We are no longer going to wait for things to happen. Now we are going to *make* things happen." And knowing there was work to do tomorrow, Allison began unpacking. If this was going to be home for a while, she might as well make her shelter comfortable.

Will the girls' plan to build a boat and rescue themselves succeed? Read Lost Girls #2: Alone!

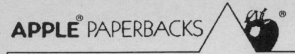

APPLE® PAPERBACKS

Pick an Apple and Polish Off Some Great Reading!

BEST-SELLING APPLE TITLES

- ❏ MT42975-2 **The Bullies and Me** Harriet Savitz — $2.75
- ❏ MT42709-1 **Christina's Ghost** Betty Ren Wright — $2.75
- ❏ MT41682-0 **Dear Dad, Love Laurie** Susan Beth Pfeffer — $2.75
- ❏ MT43461-6 **The Dollhouse Murders** Betty Ren Wright — $2.75
- ❏ MT42545-5 **Four Month Friend** Susan Clymer — $2.75
- ❏ MT43444-6 **Ghosts Beneath Our Feet** Betty Ren Wright — $2.75
- ❏ MT44351-8 **Help! I'm a Prisoner in the Library** Eth Clifford — $2.75
- ❏ MT43188-9 **The Latchkey Kids** Carol Anshaw — $2.75
- ❏ MT44567-7 **Leah's Song** Eth Clifford — $2.75
- ❏ MT43618-X **Me and Katie (The Pest)** Ann M. Martin — $2.75
- ❏ MT41529-8 **My Sister, The Creep** Candice F. Ransom — $2.75
- ❏ MT42883-7 **Sixth Grade Can Really Kill You** Barthe DeClements — $2.75
- ❏ MT40409-1 **Sixth Grade Secrets** Louis Sachar — $2.75
- ❏ MT42882-9 **Sixth Grade Sleepover** Eve Bunting — $2.75
- ❏ MT41732-0 **Too Many Murphys** Colleen O'Shaughnessy McKenna — $2.75
- ❏ MT42326-6 **Veronica the Show-Off** Nancy K. Robinson — $2.75

Available wherever you buy books, or use this order form.

Scholastic Inc., P.O. Box 7502, 2931 East McCarty Street, Jefferson City, MO 65102

Please send me the books I have checked above. I am enclosing $_____ (please add $2.00 to cover shipping and handling). Send check or money order — no cash or C.O.D.s please.

Name _____

Address _____

City_____ State/Zip _____

Please allow four to six weeks for delivery. Offer good in the U.S.A. only. Sorry, mail orders are not available to residents of Canada. Prices subject to change.

APP1090